POISONS UNKNOWN

Books by Frank Kane

POISONS
UNKNOWN

A JOHNNY LIDDELL MYSTERY

By Frank Kane

WILDSIDE PRESS

POISONS UNKNOWN

1.

THE APARTMENT was small, dark, hot.

The man in the rumpled white suit swabbed at his face with a pocket handkerchief, poured two fingers of rum into a water glass, swallowed it in a gulp. He got up, walked to the window, and stared out at the heat mist that shimmered over New Orleans and gave no evidence of relief.

He wiped the back of his neck with the handkerchief, shrugged out of his jacket. The armpits of his shirt were half-mooned with sweat; the back stuck damply to his body.

The tap on the door was so soft, he almost missed it. He cocked his head, listened. The tapping was repeated.

He crossed the floor and put his ear against the door. "What is it?" There was a faintly liquid accent in his voice.

"I have a message for you from Kirk," the voice on the other side of the door whispered.

Satisfied, the little man turned the key in the lock and pulled the door open. A man and a woman stood in the hallway. The man in the room squinted at them in the half-light.

"You were not supposed to come here," he complained.

1

"No one must know I am here." He gestured impatiently for them to come in, closed the door after them.

As he turned to face them, something in the other man's expression startled him. He looked from the man to the woman, started to back away.

"Give me the message, please. I am busy. I—"

The other man started toward him; the girl took up a position in front of the door.

The man in the white suit stared at the newcomer, recognition slowly dawning in his eyes. "You? But you said—" The words froze in his throat. His lips moved, but no sounds came. His eyes widened until they were completely rimmed with white.

"Come here," the other man ordered.

The little man moved back in horror, turned, tried to run. The other man moved faster. In two steps he was on the back of the little man, his arm around his neck in a murderous mugger's grip. As the little man struggled to break the hold, the mugger put his knee in the small of his back and bent him slowly but relentlessly back.

The victim reached up with both hands and clawed desperately at the arm that was cutting off his breath, slowly strangling him. His eyes started to pop; his struggles grew weaker. After a minute, his hands seemed to grow heavy and dropped to his sides, fingers clenching and unclenching spasmodically.

Relentlessly, the mugger tightened his grip until even the fingers stopped moving. The man in the white suit went limp. Satisfied that his victim was beyond further resistance, the mugger loosened his hold and let the little man's body slump to the floor.

The mugger stood over him, while he wiped the wet smear of his mouth with the back of his hand. The girl walked over, bent over the man on the floor, and pulled a wallet from his breast pocket. She flipped through the papers and held up a torn baggage check. "Here's half of it."

The man swore fluently. "Where's the other half?"

"Kirk must have it."

The man swore again. He brought back his foot and kicked viciously at the fallen man's head. The girl turned, walked to the door. The mugger kept kicking at the man's head until it gave off a sound like an overripe melon.

Two days later, Johnny Liddell leaned against the bar in Mike's Deadline Café in New York, staring morosely at his reflection in the back-bar mirror. It didn't look any better than he felt.

The man behind the bar made a production out of selecting a bottle from the well, filling a jigger to within a hairline of the top, and sliding it across the bar without spilling a drop.

Johnny Liddell wasn't quite as successful in transferring it to his glass.

The bartender bared the yellow stumps of his teeth in a grin, as he swabbed the bar dry with a damp cloth that left oily circles. "Takes practice, my boy."

"I should have enough of that," Liddell grunted.

The man behind the bar tossed the cloth under the bar. "Haven't been around much lately, Johnny. Business picking up?"

"Business?" Liddell made a sour face. "Playing bodyguard to some tin coffeepots at a wedding. A couple of dames who want to know where their husbands spend their evenings, a couple of husbands ditto their wives. You call that a business?"

3

"It's better than working." The bartender caught a signal from the far end of the bar and shuffled down.

Liddell took a deep swallow from his glass, while he studied the other denizens of the Deadline Café. He tried to work up some interest in the redhead at the other end of the bar who was working an overtired businessman, but decided it wasn't worth the trouble. He finished his drink, spilled some change next to it, and turned up the collar of his topcoat.

The bartender shuffled back, scooped up the money. "One for the road, Johnny? On the house."

Liddell considered it, decided no amount of liquor would shake him out of the mood he was in, shook his head.

The cool breeze flapping the awnings of some of the fancier *boîtes* along Madison Avenue felt good after the closeness of the bar. He looked up at the sky and decided it was a good night for walking. He was halfway up the block when the man came up behind him and tapped him on the shoulder.

"I thought you was never going to come out, Liddell," a nasal voice whined accusingly. "A guy could catch his death of cold in this damn climate."

Liddell looked him over in the yellow street light. He was thin and undersized, a fact that the carefully tailored gabardine, built-up shoulders, and elevator shoes failed to conceal. He wore no hat; a mass of thick black hair rolled back in oily waves from his low hairline. He wore it in a three-quarter part revealing the startling whiteness of his scalp. His thin, bloodless lips were split in what was intended to be a smile, but there was no trace of it in the eyes that squinted across the high bridge of an enormous hooked nose.

Over his right arm he carried a carefully folded top-

4

coat. The ugly snout of a .45 poked out from under its folds.

"What's on your mind, friend?"

"I just came by to invite you to a party."

Liddell's eyes dropped to the .45. "You make it hard to refuse such hospitality. But give me a rain check on this one. I'm not dressed for a party."

The thin lips tilted at the corners, and the eyes grew bleaker. "You are for this one. It's a come-as-you-are party."

"Who's throwing it?"

"What do you take me for, a stool pigeon?" Without taking his eyes off Liddell, the little man raised his hand in a signal. A big black sedan pulled away from the curb down the block and glided toward them. It came to a noiseless stop at the curb, and the back door swung open. The little man motioned with the .45. "Be my guest."

Liddell debated the advisibility of making a fight for it, dropped the decision. "You talked me into it." He stepped in and dropped back against the cushions.

The man with the gun followed him in, closing the door after him. He settled back in his corner, with the .45 cradled in the crook of his elbow. Its muzzle stared at Liddell's midsection.

"Have we got far to go?" Liddell wanted to know.

The little man shrugged. "Depends on how much traffic we hit in the tunnel." He took a flat platinum case from his pocket and held it out. "Smoke?"

Liddell selected one of the long, thin cigarettes, smelled it, shook his head. "I prefer tobacco in mine."

The man with the gun shrugged. "After a day like this has been, I can use a lift." He stuck one of the long cigarettes in the corner of his mouth, motioned with

5

the .45. "Get one of your own if you like. But just use two fingers in bringing it out."

"I'm not heeled if that's what's worrying you."

The little man pasted the frosty grin back on his lips. "Who's worrying? I'm just careful. Use more than two fingers and I'll blast the hand off."

Liddell fished in his jacket pocket with thumb and forefinger, brought up a pack of cigarettes. He shook one loose and replaced the pack. "Heading for Jersey, eh? Anyone I know?"

"There you go, trying to spoil the surprise again," the little man chided. He leaned over, touched a lighter to Liddell's cigarette, returned to his corner. "You'll find out soon enough."

Liddell shrugged and settled back, smoking moodily. The big car emerged on the Jersey side of the Holland Tunnel, headed for the Pulaski Skyway. The driver handled the car as if it were a scooter, cutting in and out of the crawling traffic, making time. Once past the Newark Airport, he bore right toward Union, swung onto Route 29.

The character of the neighborhood changed from densely populated to suburban, with bigger and bigger stretches of unpopulated areas showing up. About forty minutes from the Holland Tunnel, the driver swung off 29 onto a macadam road that meandered back about a mile.

"Club Coronet, eh?" Liddell asked.

The little man's teeth flashed whitely in the gloom. "You do know your way around. I told you we were going to a party."

"Lew Crossan behind this?" Liddell growled.

"That punk?" There was contempt in the little man's

6

voice. "You think I'd be running errands for him?" He snorted audibly, then relapsed into an injured silence.

From the outside, the Club Coronet gave no hint of its character but looked like any other estate that had been kept up. The lawn and shrubs were in good condition, and it was only by the small brass name plate on the stone pillars that it could be identified.

The big car swung between the pillars and headed up a bluestone driveway that wound and curved its way through a row of trees to the house itself.

"Know where the office is?"

"Still upstairs?"

The little man nodded. "That's where we're going. Make it easy on yourself. I'll be right behind you." He brandished the .45. "So will Betsy."

The car pulled up to a canopied entrance. The little man got out first, waited for Liddell, then followed him up the broad stone staircase. A grilled metal door led into what obviously had once been a reception hall.

Small groups of people in formal dress were clustered all through the hall. A low murmur of polite conversation welled toward Liddell as he walked in. Overhead a pall of smoke stirred restlessly in the draft from the opened door.

Liddell headed for the staircase at the far end of the hall; the little man trotted along at his heels.

The door at the head of the stairs had the word "Private" stenciled on it in gold leaf. The little man turned the knob, pushed the door open.

A man sat on the corner of a desk that looked as if it had cost important money, his feet swinging lightly against the side. He didn't look up from the engrossing task of paring his fingernails.

"Here's Liddell, boss."

"Took you long enough, Hook."

"I couldn't get to him, boss. He was in a bar with a lot of people. I had to wait until he came out, didn't I? I damn near froze." The little man sounded as if he were on the verge of crying. "I got him here soon's I could."

"Go down to the bar and get something to warm you up. I'll call you if I need you."

The little man nodded, turned, and scooted out the door.

The man on the desk looked up. "Hello, Liddell. Remember me?"

Liddell studied the man's features, then nodded. "Marty Kirk."

"Nice of you to come all the way out here to see me," Kirk snapped the blade of his knife closed and dropped it into his pocket.

"You mean I had a choice?"

Kirk chuckled. "That Hook, he never learns. You tell him to bring somebody, he only knows one thing." He got off the edge of the desk, walked around, sat behind it. "Been a long time, Liddell. Must be four, five years."

"Five."

The years had made a lot of changes in Kirk, Liddell realized. The lean wolfishness of his face was blurred by a soft overlay of fat. Flat, lusterless eyes still peered from beneath heavily veined, thickened eyelids, but the soft discolored pouches beneath them took away the old menace.

"I need a boy, Liddell. I came up personally to offer you the job." Kirk reached into the lower drawer and brought up a bottle and two glasses. "Before you say anything, it's strictly legit."

"Where is this job? Here?"

8

"You know my territory's the bayou country. I just borrowed this place from Crossan because I don't want word out that I'm in town. It's personal business." He uncorked the bottle, spilled some liquor into each of the glasses. "Listening?"

Liddell took one of the glasses. "Listening," he said.

"Take a look at these." He pulled a batch of stapled clippings from his pocket and tossed them across the desk. Liddell picked them up, riffled through them, read snatches.

"So?"

"Interesting?"

"Fascinating. So what? Some guy running a Holy Roller show in New Orleans blasts hell out of you in the newspapers. He's against sin. So?"

Kirk looked up. "He's disappeared."

"So what?"

"I want him found."

Liddell shook his head. "It's still like the old days, Kirk. I don't bird-dog anybody for a hit."

Kirk shook his head. "It ain't like that, Liddell. Anything happens to him, I'm sunk. That's why I've got to find him before something does."

"Why?"

"Don't you get it? He's been tearing the hide off me and my operation in the newspapers. He disappears, somebody gets the idea I had him hit, the heat goes on. Him calling me names don't mean anything. But if anything happens to him, there's plenty heat."

Liddell tasted his drink, approved. "Good stuff."

"Private stock. Not the varnish they pour down there." He tasted his drink, emptied his glass. "Well?"

"You think this character's been snatched?"

"What pro would pull a job like that?" Kirk snorted.

9

"This guy's playing house with one of the dames that fall for that yogi routine of his, and if the papers ever get their hooks into it, we're cooked."

Liddell shook his head. "It doesn't sound kosher to me, Kirk."

"Maybe this will convince you I'm leveling," Kirk leaned back in the desk chair, put the sole of his shoe against the edge of the desk. "Remember a little blonde named Gabby Benton?" He outlined an hourglass with his hands.

Liddell grinned. "Sure, I remember Gabby. She still running her detective agency down there?"

Kirk nodded. "I hired her agency to find this creep. She's got the only outfit down there I trust. She can't swing it alone. You'll be working with her on it."

"This Gabby's idea?"

Kirk shrugged. "She says you're the only op in the country can find this guy fast enough to keep it out of the papers. She won't come up and ask you to work with her. So I did." He pulled out his wallet, riffled through a wad of bills. "There's five gees in it for each of you if you find him."

Johnny Liddell looked out the window at the cold, wind-swept November evening, compared it to the tropical warmth of New Orleans. Mentally, he tried to compute how many tin coffeepots he would have to guard and how many suspicious spouses would have to be told how their other half loves to make five thousand. The tin coffeepots, the suspicious spouses, and the northern climate dropped the decision.

2.

THE SUN was shining brightly when Johnny Liddell got off the DC-6 in New Orleans. He stood at the head of the debarking platform, squinting into the slanting sunlight. Gabby Benton was behind the fence near the exit gate. She spotted him at almost the same moment he saw her, and waved.

She shouldered her way through the cluster at the gate and ran to meet him. From close she didn't look a day older. Her skin was still a smooth cocoa tan. Her hair was silky and gold, caught up in a soft bun on the nape of her neck. She wore a loose-fitting silk peasant blouse that did nothing to discount her assets. There was a faint blue color under her eyes that supplemented their deep blue color.

Her lips were full, moist. She hadn't forgotten how to kiss.

Johnny Liddell held her out at arm's length, ran his eyes from the molten gleam of her hair to her ballet slippers with appropriate stops on the way. "You sure look good, baby. You haven't changed a bit."

"You're a liar, but I love it." The blonde grinned. "But you really haven't changed. You're two hours late. Five years have passed and here I am still waiting for Liddell."

Liddell caught her by the arm, headed for the exit gate. "Don't give me that. Waiting for Liddell," he snorted. "You got yourself married before I hardly got out of town."

"Oh, that one," she dismissed it airily. "That was just to show you I didn't care that you were walking out on me." She pointed to a light blue Cadillac convertible in the parking lot. "Want to drive?"

"In this town? Not if I'm in my right mind," he shook his head. "If I tried to drive that tank down Bourbon Street, I'd scrape the fenders against the houses on both sides." He tossed his bag into the back seat, slid into the front.

The blonde groaned. "Don't tell me you're going to stay at that flea bag?"

"The Delcort, if you don't mind, driver."

"You remember how broken down it was last time you were here? Well, it was in first-class shape then compared to the way it is now. Why do you want to go there?"

"Sentiment. Pure sentiment. It brings back my youth."

Gabby slid behind the wheel. "I've got plenty of room at my place."

Liddell grinned. "I didn't mean it brings back my youth exactly. I meant it brings back memories of my youth."

The blonde muttered under her breath, stabbed at the starter button on the dash, raced the engine to a roar, let it settle back to a purr. "I'm beginning to wonder if it was worth all the trouble to connive you back to New Orleans. The town's already full of old men." She eased the car out of the lot and swung onto the state highway.

"What's the real pitch on this Brother Alfred deal?"

12

Gabby shrugged. "The usual. He runs this so-called temple for a bunch of the local cutups. Gets away with murder, but they keep hands off because he seems to know too many right people."

"Sort of a Holy Roller deal, eh?"

"Worse. Alfred's a cross between Marie Laveau and Malvina Latour. Some of those prayer meetings of his would make a voodoo turn white."

"Sounds interesting," Liddell grunted.

"You'll see one tonight. I made a contact with Angie Martinez. She's one of Alfred's pets. She's going to pass us in." She swung the big car around a slow-moving airport bus, pushed the accelerator to the floor. The big car leaped away, ate up the miles toward the center of town. "It'll give you something to write in your diary."

"Your boy Kirk really interested in finding Alfred or is he using us to bird-dog him for a kill?"

Gabby shrugged. "It figures that the heat will really be on if anything happens to Alfred. He's been getting a lot of space lately blasting Marty. I don't think Marty would take the chance of having anything happen to him."

"Any idea on what did happen to him?"

The blonde wrinkled her nose. "My guess is that he's playing house with one of his flock, and he'll turn up when he's good and ready. He's got a pretty ripe reputation."

"Then how come the papers have been giving his blasts against Marty so much space?"

"Everybody's against sin. And Alfred's good copy. Walks around in flowing white robes and all that sort of thing. Makes Aimee Semple MacPherson look as colorless as an albino on a snow pile."

Gabby swung the car onto Canal, headed uptown.

13

"What's my status with the police in this town, Gabby?"

"You're all set. I registered you at City Hall as connected with my agency. They issued a thirty-day license and gun permit. It's renewable."

Liddell grinned. "O.K., boss. What's the first thing on the calendar?"

"What would the Chamber of Commerce think of me if I didn't insist on the Blue Room to take the dust out of your throat?" She threaded the big car through the traffic on Canal, turned off on Baronne, braked to a stop in front of the Hotel Roosevelt. A big black man in an admiral's uniform came running down the steps, opened the door.

"There are some bags in the back, Nick," Gabby told him. "Have a boy run them over to the Delcort on Bourbon Street and register Mr. Liddell in, will you?"

The doorman's white teeth gleamed brightly in a broad grin. "Doggone, ef it ain't. You goin' be with us long, Mr. Johnny?"

"Depends, Nick."

The doorman shook his head, grinned. "You better stay around till Mister Weiss gets back from his trip. He awful mad if'n he miss you."

Liddell slipped a folded bill into the man's hand and led Gabby up the short flight of steps into the hotel.

The Blue Room was dim, cool, intimate after the heat of the street. Johnny Liddell told the waiter to bring two Ramos and two bourbon and settled back.

"Doesn't feel as if I've ever been away. Nothing ever changes much, does it?" The waiter deposited two frothy white drinks in front of them, laid two jiggers of bourbon alongside them.

Liddell took a swallow from the white drink and made

14

a face. "I never could work up a taste for that stuff. Take it away," he told the waiter.

Gabby frowned at him. "What was that all about? What did you order it for in the first place?"

"For five years I've been trying to remember what it tasted like." He washed the sweet taste from his mouth with the bourbon. "Now I remember why I don't like it."

"How are we going to tackle this Brother Alfred chore, Johnny? Marty expects action, and he gets pretty nasty when he's disappointed." She fumbled in the depths of her handbag and came up with a pack of cigarettes.

"Fill me in on this guy. How long's he been operating? What's his graft?"

Gabby lit two cigarettes and held one out to Liddell. "I've got a whole file on him over at my place. Nobody knows where he came from. He showed up here about five years ago. Started this Eye Almighty cult. First just the frustrated old dames who fall for any racket like that flocked around. But then, when word got around, it became fashionable to be a member."

"How's it operating with him out of the picture?"

"He's got a high priestess. A big full-blown gal named Wanda. She's been standing in for him. You'll get a chance to see her in action tonight. I understand she's real gone."

Liddell emptied the second jigger of bourbon. "Any line on her?"

Gabby shook her head. "Rumors around are that she's a New Orleans octoroon, but I've never been able to nail it down."

"How about the cops in this burg? They used to be pretty tough on that kind of operation."

"The temple is just across the parish line. And you know how some of the parish sheriffs are down here."

15

She finished her drink. "Want to go up to my place and look over the file?"

Liddell took a last drag on the cigarette and snubbed it out in the ash tray. He pulled a wallet from his pocket and dropped three bills on the table. "Living in the same place?"

Gabby shook her head. "I moved over to this side of Canal a year or so ago. Not as picturesque as your side, but more livable." She pushed back her chair and stood up. "When a gal gets to twenty-five, she's willing to trade quaintness for comfort."

Gabby Benton's place turned out to be an elaborately furnished apartment in one of the expensive cliff dwellings that had sprung up along Carondolet and all throughout the modern area of New Orleans since the end of the war. She led the way through a cluttered foyer into a cheerfully furnished combination living room and den. She pushed a pile of papers off the settee onto the coffee table, dropping her handbag on top of them.

"There's some pretty fair rye and Scotch in the decanters, and I've got some real old bourbon hidden under the bed. What'll it be?"

"Bourbon."

The blonde nodded. "You get the ice and water. I'll get the bourbon." She disappeared in the direction of the bedroom.

Liddell wandered out to the kitchen, found a bowl, filled it with ice. He brought the ice and a pitcher of water back to the coffee table and set them down.

The bedroom door opened; Gabby handed a bottle out. "Make the drinks, Johnny. I'll be out as soon as I freshen up."

16

Liddell took the bottle, dropped some ice into each glass, drenched it down with bourbon. He added a touch of water, swished the liquor over the ice. "Now I remember why I left this town. It's an oven," he called in.

"Take off your jacket and be comfortable. I intend to be."

Liddell shrugged out of the jacket and draped it over the back of his chair. He sniffed at his glass, approved, took a deep swallow. It tasted as good as it smelled. He was just refilling his glass when the door opened and Gabby came in.

She had changed her blouse and skirt for a housecoat of clinging blue material. Her yellow hair was piled on top of her head, her face looked as though it had been freshly scrubbed. She wore no make-up except a smear of lipstick.

"Let's take the drinks and the makings out to the sun deck," she suggested. "That's the only place we'll get a breath of air."

She led the way through a French door to a porch that seemed to be pasted to the side of the building with no apparent support from below. It had a gaily colored awning that protected it from the sun and the curious above, and fan-shaped, opaque glass guard screens that guaranteed it privacy from neighbors on either side.

Liddell looked around, staring out through the heat mist that seemed to be settling over the city. "This is all right. The private-eye business must be good down these parts."

Gabby shrugged. "It's a living." She dropped onto a large divan drawn against the side of the building, drew her knees up under her. "The apartment is the only thing I got out of my brief plunge into matrimony." When she leaned back, her breasts strained against the

17

fabric, threatening the seams. "I suppose you know that I always blamed you for the bust-up of my marriage?" She sipped at her glass.

"Me? What are you talking about? I was a couple of thousand miles away."

Gabby nodded. "I know. But you spoiled me for other men." She leaned forward and raised her half-parted lips to him, seemingly unaware that the front of her housecoat had sagged open with breath-taking effect.

When he covered her lips with his, she shuddered deliciously, drew away. She studied him with half-closed eyes and bit at her lower lip.

"I read all about you and that newspaper girl, too, Johnny." She patted the couch at her side. "It sounded serious."

Liddell dropped down beside her, shrugged. "Muggsy's a swell kid. But a guy in my racket has no right to ask any gal to share the risks."

The blonde put her hand on his knee. "I'm in the same racket." She turned the full power of her eyes on him, then grinned. "O.K., Liddell. I'm not trying to make an honest man out of you. One fling at matrimony proved it's not for me, either." She took a deep swallow from her glass. "I guess we're two of a kind."

"Discouraging, ain't it?" Liddell grinned.

She drained her glass and held it out for a refill. When he handed it to her, she set it down on the floor next to the couch, swung her feet up, lay back in his lap. She caught him by the tie, pulled his mouth down to hers. After a moment, her arms slid around his neck, her nails dug into his shoulder. Her lips moved against his.

The phone in the living room started to jangle. Liddell straightened up, glowering at it.

Gabby made a halfhearted effort to pull the robe to-

18

gether over the broad expanse of flesh it revealed, but gave it up as a bad try. She looked at Liddell and chuckled. "You look good in lipstick. My lipstick." She touched her lips lightly to his, swung her legs off the couch, walked in to the phone.

Her round hips worked smooth and easy under the thin fabric of the gown. When she returned a few seconds later, the effect was as satisfying from the front as it had been from the rear.

"That was Martinez, Johnny. The gal that's going to sneak us into the temple tonight. We're to be at the back door at nine." She consulted her watch. "It's almost six now."

Liddell handed her her drink, staring up at her. "Three hours."

The blonde took a sip, studied him over the rim of her glass. "Think you'll be bored waiting?"

He got up, stood close to her. "I never used to be, baby." He grinned crookedly.

She pressed against him, found his mouth with hers. After a moment he started to pull away. She shook her head frantically, sank her teeth into his lower lip. When she finally drew back, her lips were moist, soft, her eyes glazed.

"I've been waiting for you a long time, Johnny," she told him huskily. "Five long years."

She slid out of his arms, shrugged her shoulders free of the gown. It slid down past her knees, and she stepped out of it. Her breasts were firm, full, pink-tipped, her waist trim and narrow. Her legs were long, tapering pillars; her stomach flat and firm.

"Maybe we can turn the calendar back," she whispered.

She slid back into his arms, melted against him. As

19

his lips found her half-open mouth her nails dug spasmodically into his shoulders. She emitted little animal cries deep in her chest, quivering uncontrollably.

Liddell kissed her cheeks, her closed eyes, the lobes of her ears.

"You'll never know how much I've wanted you. How very much," she breathed heavily.

He got a pretty good idea.

3.

THE EYE ALMIGHTY TABERNACLE was four miles from downtown New Orleans, just across the line in San Vincente Parish. Gabby nosed the big convertible past the row of ramshackle frame buildings that clustered on the parish line, and headed for the open country beyond. After a few minutes' drive, she swung the big convertible off the state road onto a macadam road that wandered back through a clump of trees.

After a moment, the car's headlights picked up the boarded-up windows of an old paint-peeled white house.

"You sure this is the place, Gabby?" Liddell grunted.

"What do you want, neon lights and a brass band?" The blonde guided the big car around the building and stopped in a weed-choked parking space in the back. There were a dozen or more other cars huddled there in the darkness. Gabby cut her motor and lights. She snapped on her dash light, consulted a tiny baguette on her wrist.

"Pretty nearly on the head. Eight fifty-five. Let's go."

They walked over to a door set in the rear of the building and knocked. The door creaked open, spilled a long yellow triangle of light that seemed to spread across the yard toward the cars.

21

"Gabby?" A girl asked in a low voice.

"Yeah."

They stepped in through the door, shut it behind them. The girl was small, mousy. Her eyes seemed to pop as she studied Liddell; her upper teeth were painfully prominent. She pushed a wisp of mousy hair out of her face, tucked it untidily into place behind her ear. She was dressed in a flowing white gown that reached to the floor.

"Be careful, will you, Gabby?" she pleaded. "If Wanda ever found out I passed you through, she'd give me a hard time."

Gabby nodded. "We'll be careful, Angie." She motioned for Liddell to follow her, led the way through what was obviously once a big kitchen, now unused, dust-ridden. As they crossed the butler's pantry, Liddell became aware of a dull, monotonous beat that made the old place vibrate.

From the pantry, a long corridor ran to the front of the house where a heavy, black-velvet drape sealed off the parlor beyond. In the corridor the monotonous beat was identifiable as the pounding of a drum.

Gabby stopped Liddell at the drape with a tug on the arm. "Just melt into the back of the crowd," she cautioned. "Nobody'll notice."

She pushed back the curtain; they slid through. As they entered the room beyond, the wild beat of the music poured over them, enveloped them with almost physical force.

The ceiling and the floor to the room above had been torn out making the room huge, two-storied. Heavy drapes covered the walls from floor to ceiling, and on the floor a thick pile rug completed the soundproofing.

At the far end of the room there was a small dais;

over it a tremendous eye had been painted in luminous paint. It seemed to glare down with personal malice, follow their every move.

The room was bathed in a dim light that transformed the faces of the people scattered around it into leering gargoyles. There was no furniture, but men and women of all ages were draped on cushions scattered around the floor. No one even looked up as Liddell and Gabby entered and found some space in the corner of the room.

Soon, a cleverly disguised door to the left of the dais opened; two young *café-au-lait* colored girls came out, their heads wrapped up in the traditional *tignon*.

They spread a small tablecloth in the center of the room and placed lighted tallow candles at the corners of it. As a centerpiece, they put down a shallow woven basket filled with herbs, and scattered little white beans and corn around the basket.

An old Negro stood in the corner, astride a cylinder made of staves hooped with brass and headed with sheepskin. With two sticks he started up the monotonous deep-throated beat they had noticed in the corridor. Keeping time with him, another Negro was sawing away at a two-stringed fiddle. It had a long neck, a body about three inches in diameter that was covered with a brightly mottled snakeskin. The third member of this primitive orchestra twirled a long calabash, made of a native gourd filled with pebbles.

The door alongside the dais opened again, and a tall woman came out. She wore a long scarlet robe; her black hair cascaded down over her shoulders. She walked with a peculiar gliding motion, ascended the dais, started to chant a wild sort of ritual song.

"That's Wanda," Gabby whispered.

Liddell nodded, keeping his eyes on the scarlet-robed

woman. As she sang, she seemed to grow in stature; her eyes began to roll in wild frenzy. Her head started to bob in time with the chant and the primitive wail of the two-stringed fiddle.

The others in the room took up the beat, started to sway in unison, keep time with their hands and feet. One by one they picked up the chant, their bodies swaying in time to the weird and savagely monotonous rhythm of the gourd and drum.

The woman in the scarlet gown increased the tempo; the room became charged with electricity. Suddenly, one of the women let out a little scream, jumped to the middle of the floor, started to twist and dance with wild abandon. One of the young colored girls joined her on the floor, started to parade around with a strangely stamping motion. The beat deepened in intensity.

As the girl in the *tignon* passed the tablecloth, she grabbed the candles and marched with them in her hands. The white woman followed her. Soon others got up, joined the march around the room.

As the young Negro girl reached the dais, the woman in the scarlet robe gave her a drink out of a gourd. She swallowed some, spat the rest in a mist, holding the candles so as to catch the vapor. The alcohol blazed up in a blinding flare. There was a roar from all parts of the room.

Others jumped to their feet, commenced to move in a circle. The woman on the dais continued to increase the tempo and handed the gourd to each of the dancers as they passed.

The posturing and contortions became more and more abandoned as the dancers circled the tablecloth. From time to time they would reach over, pick up the herbs

24

from the basket or a handful of the white beans or corn, and chew on them.

A young woman sprang from the line of marchers and jumped on the cloth in the center of the floor. Her body started to undulate from shoulders to hips to ankles. The beat of the drum, the scream of the fiddle swelled in volume; her motions became more and more abandoned. Wildly, she tore at her clothes, ripped them from her body. She danced wildly, her hair flying, her body undulating and throbbing in time with the music. Her motions became more and more frantic until suddenly, with a wild scream, she collapsed in a heap on the floor and lay there.

That was a signal for the whole line of marchers to take up her dance. The drumbeat speeded up in intensity; the motions of the dancers kept time. The women tore at their clothes, and entirely nude, went on dancing.

Suddenly, the candles went out, the dim light that bathed the room faded. Only a spotlight picked out the woman in the scarlet gown on the dais. Her eyes were closed; she seemed in a trance.

"Now what?" Liddell whispered.

"You let your conscience be your guide. We'd better get out of here while the lights are out." Gabby's voice sounded shaken, and her hand was damp to the touch.

Liddell followed her to the heavy curtain that sealed off the room, slid through. They traversed the corridor and slipped out the back door.

The warm night air seemed chilly after the super-heated atmosphere of the orgy they had just left. They crossed to the Caddy. Gabby started it, eased it around the house, and headed for the road.

"Well, what do you think about it?" she asked finally.

Liddell wiped his upper lip with the side of his hand. "It's not exactly a way to grow old gracefully, is it?" He deflected the wind stream and leaned back, letting the cool breeze blow the bad taste from his mouth. "How long does it go on?"

"Maybe an hour." She guided the big car back to the state road. "Now what?"

"Is there a place around here where we can kill an hour or so? Maybe have a drink?"

"I think there's a roadhouse up the road. Just inside the parish line." She headed for it, eying Liddell curiously. "What's perking on the inside of that skull of yours?"

Liddell shrugged. "I figure on going back to the temple after the party's over. I've got a yen to have a little talk with that black-haired babe that did the chanting."

"Wanda? Quite a hunk of woman, eh?"

"Quite a hunk." Liddell nodded and lapsed into silence.

A few minutes' drive brought them to a large rambling roadhouse set back off the main road. A flickering neon that dyed the branches of the trees and the surrounding lawn red identified it as "The Hideaway." Gabby pulled the Caddy into a pebbled parking space and led the way in.

They found a booth near the back of the bar and squeezed in.

A bored-looking waitress shuffled over, dropped menus in front of them, but didn't seem terribly disconcerted when they told her they just wanted a drink. After she had shuffled back in the direction of the bar, Liddell dumped a pack of cigarettes on the table.

"Ever join in that May dance they do, Gabby?" He hung a cigarette in the corner of his mouth.

The girl selected a cigarette, bent forward, accepted a light. "Once, just for kicks." She took a deep drag, let the smoke dribble from her nostrils. "It really gets into your blood. It took days before I could even see straight."

Liddell nodded. "What's in the bottle she gives you to drink?"

"Some kind of wine. It's sweet tasting, plenty strong."

Liddell grunted. "Probably spiked with hashish. That gang back there's higher than the Empire State Building." He leaned back, let the waitress slide two glasses and two shots in front of them, and waited until she had left. "I don't know where the pay-off is yet, but it looks to me as if the Eye Almighty is just a fancy dope drop."

Gabby made a *moue*, studying the carmined end of her cigarette with distaste. "Seems like an awfully complicated way to sell dope. Why go to all that trouble when an addict will save you the trouble by looking you up?"

"What better way to make new customers?"

Gabby considered it. "You think that's what's behind the Eye Almighty?" She shrugged. "Funny nobody has blown a whistle on them. You don't become an addict just by using the stuff once."

Liddell tasted his drink and approved. "How do you figure the candles being put out after the wild dancing?"

Gabby grinned. "Maybe in deference to the tender sensibilities of any members who aren't high, they figure the scene should be blacked out to give the others time to get their breath back."

"Ever hear of a snooperscope, Gabby?"

The blonde scowled, shook her head. "What is it?"

"They developed it during the last war. It's used for observations in the dark. Uses infrared." He took a deep drag on the cigarette, blew the smoke in twin streams from his nostrils. "Anybody in that room with a snooperscope could see everything that was going on as clearly as if the lights were on."

"I'll bet he was blushing."

"No, but tomorrow some of those people probably will be. You can also use infrared to take flashlight pictures or even movies in the pitch dark. And the flash never shows!"

Gabby's mouth formed a perfect O of awakening. "I see what you mean. That's the reason there's no kickback on the orgies and the reason they keep coming back until they're hooked?"

Liddell nodded, scowling at the glowing tip of his cigarette. "You said it was pretty hard to get into the Temple?"

Gabby nodded. "Plenty hard. It's more exclusive than most clubs." She chewed on the end of a lacquered fingernail. "You think Alfred is already dead? One of his flock that he's been shaking down maybe?"

"It could be, but I doubt it, Gabby," Liddell shook his head. "Anybody weak enough to get sucked into a setup like that is usually too weak to blast his way out. He's usually more prone to buy his way out." He drained his glass and signaled for a refill.

"You think Wanda knows anything?" Gabby asked.

Liddell shrugged. "She must have some idea of whether he has any enemies or not. When you work as closely with somebody as she's been working with Alfred, you have a pretty good idea of what cooks."

"Maybe."

"Another thing. So far as I can see, nobody has a picture of this character or any way to identify him. She may be able to help in that department, too." He took a last deep drag on his butt and chain-lit a fresh one from it. "You've seen him. What's he look like?"

Gabby pursed her lips. "He's hard to describe."

"Tall?"

"Fairly tall."

Liddell sighed. "How tall? Taller than I am?"

Gabby cocked her head, studied Liddell's heavy-set shoulders, the thick, gray-flecked hair, and made a helpless gesture. "I don't know. He always wore a white gown. Makes it hard to tell."

"All right. Skip his height. What would you say he weighed?"

She shook her head. "I don't have any idea."

"See what I mean? Go on, describe the rest of him."

Gabby screwed up her forehead and grimaced in concentration. "He was bald, wore a heavy black beard, black-rimmed glasses." She racked her brain and finally shook her head. "That's all I can remember about him," she confessed.

Liddell grunted. "That makes it a snap. All I have to do is look for a guy who might be shorter or taller than I am. He could weigh anywhere from a hundred to two hundred pounds, he has a beard he could shave off, a bald head he could cover, and horn-rimmed glasses that could be changed into steel-rimmed glasses just by walking into an optometrist's. Yes, sir. Finding him should be a breeze!"

4.

At 12:25, Johnny Liddell climbed the rickety front steps of the Eye Almighty Temple. There was no sign of life anywhere in the building. He rapped on the door with the old-fashioned brass knocker.

After a moment, the door opened a patch. The painfully prominent front teeth of Angie Martinez gleamed in the half-light. She stared at him as if she had never seen him before, and seemed to have difficulty focusing her eyes on his face.

"The services are over." Her voice was low, melodious.

"I want to talk to Sister Wanda. About Brother Alfred."

The girl frowned as if she were trying to remember something important. She shook her head mechanically. "Brother Alfred has been taken from us."

"I have come to bring him back. I must see Sister Wanda."

The girl wrestled with it, then opened the door wider. "I will tell her." She pointed to the entrance to the parlor. "You will wait in there." When she left, Liddell had the illusion that she melted into the gloom of the lower hall.

The parlor was empty. There was no sign of the orgy that he had witnessed there less than two hours before.

30

The Eye continued to glare down at him with disconcertingly direct gaze.

He was mentally debating the advisability of smoking in the Presence, when he became aware of a subtle rustling sound. The woman in the scarlet robe materialized in the gloom next to the dais. She walked up to him with the peculiar gliding motion he had noticed earlier, and stopped in front of him.

"I am Sister Wanda. You wished to see me?" She had a deep, richly liquid voice. From close her face was startlingly beautiful. Her eyes were almond-shaped and green, but the pupils were so dilated they seemed black. Her hair was thick, blue black, cascading over her shoulders. Her mouth was full, sensuous, her nose thin, patrician. She wore no make-up, and her skin was the color of old ivory.

Liddell nodded. "About Brother Alfred."

The woman's eyes narrowed slightly. "Are you from the police?"

Liddell shook his head. "My name's Liddell. I'm a private investigator. I've been hired to help find the missing man."

"By whom?"

"I'm not at liberty to divulge my client, unfortunately."

The woman's lips straightened out to a thin line. "Why should you expect me to help you if you won't answer my questions?"

Liddell shrugged. "Because I thought you were interested in seeing Brother Alfred returned unharmed. Of course, if you're not—"

"What do you want to know?"

"Couldn't we talk in private?"

"We are alone. There is no one in the temple but Martinez. She won't disturb us." She followed his gaze to

31

the Eye, made a production of facing it, bowing reverently. "You need fear no intrusion from the Almighty Eye, Mr.—"

"Liddell. Johnny Liddell." He pinched at his nostrils with thumb and forefinger. "There must be some place we can talk that's a little less like Union Station?"

Sister Wanda pursed her lips. "Brother Alfred's study, perhaps. Will you please follow me?" She turned, made her obeisance to the Eye, led the way to the door set in the wall next to the dais. The room beyond was a barely furnished cell, containing an old unpainted desk, several chairs, and a bookcase piled with books. Two candles set on either end of the desk provided the illumination, spilling a flickering light into all but the corners of the room.

The woman took the chair behind the desk and folded her hands in her lap. "We won't be interrupted here."

Liddell pulled up a wooden armchair and dropped into it. "O.K. to smoke?"

The woman behind the desk nodded but shook her head when he held the pack out to her. She watched him narrowly as he hung one from the corner of his mouth, scratched a match, lit it. "What is it you want to know?"

"You've been with him long?"

The woman's eyes glowed in the candlelight. She shrugged. "Five years. Since the temple was opened."

"What about before he opened the temple? What did he do? Where did he come from?"

"Why should that concern you, Mr. Liddell?" Her voice was cold.

Liddell shrugged. "Maybe his disappearance stems out of something in his past. Somebody or something he was running away from."

32

"Brother Alfred did not run away from things."

"Then you think it was abduction?"

The woman nodded sharply. "He never would have left his work of his own free will."

Liddell smoked for a second, studying the woman's face. It told him nothing. "Who would want him abducted?"

"The underworld."

"That covers a lot of our population. Anybody in particular in the underworld?"

"A man named Kirk. He runs most of the underworld in this state. Brother Alfred had devoted himself to destroying Kirk and what he stood for."

"That could get to be fatal," Liddell conceded. "Anything else?"

Liddell snapped his fingers. "I almost forgot. A picture. I don't even know what he looked like."

"There is no picture. In this sect, we do not succumb to such petty vanities."

"That makes it tough." Liddell sighed, blew a stream of feathery gray smoke at the two-story ceiling, and watched it swirl. "Can you think of any other reason why he might disappear? A personal reason? A woman, perhaps?"

The woman's face became a dull red with anger. "You are insulting. You had better leave now. The way you talk, I get the idea you're more interested in finding some explanation for his disappearance than in finding him."

Liddell shrugged, dropped his cigarette to the floor, and ground it out. "Sorry if I hurt your feelings. In this racket you've got to explore every possibility." He pulled himself to his feet. "In other words, you have nothing to add, no suggestions?"

33

The woman shook her head coldly.

Liddell tugged a notebook and fountain pen from his breast pocket, made a few notes. "I won't bother you again." He flipped the notebook shut, started to recap the pen. His fingernail caught the refill level, shot a stream of ink out over his hand.

"Clumsy of me," he growled. "Any place I can wash it off?"

The woman snorted her annoyance, then shrugged. "There's a washroom over there." She watched him walk to the door and close it.

Once in the washroom, he worked fast. He turned on the water in the tap, opened the medicine closet. There was the usual assortment of bottles and tubes, shaving accessories, no comb or brush.

In the corner was a glass. Liddell placed his fingers on the inside of the glass, spread them open, and lifted it. Then, taking his pocket handkerchief, he wrapped it carefully. He stuck the glass in the crown of his hat and held it secure with one finger. After he'd washed the ink off, he returned to the study.

The woman greeted him with a frosty smile. "I hope there's nothing else?"

Liddell shook his head. "If anything occurs to you that you think I should know, I'm staying at the Delcort in the Vieux Carré."

The smile was still pasted on the woman's lips. It didn't reach her eyes. "I don't think there'll be any reason for me to get in touch with you." She turned on her heel and led the way to the door. She waited until he had stepped out onto the stoop, then slammed the door behind him. As he walked down the steps, he could hear the chains being put into place.

The Hotel Delcort was an old, weather-beaten, stone building that lay snuggled in a row of similarly weather-beaten stone buildings a few blocks uptown from the Old Absinthe House on Bourbon Street. Hand-hammered wrought-iron grilles decorated the small balconies outside each room with a delicate embroidery. A small metal plaque next to the doorway dispelled any possible doubts as to its character by labeling it clearly as a hotel.

A threadbare and faded carpet ran the length of the lobby that had long since given up any pretense of serving a useful purpose. The chairs were rickety, unsafe, uninviting. The imitation rubber plants were grimed with dust.

A dispirited-looking clerk presided over the desk. As Johnny Liddell walked in, the clerk raised rheumy eyes and worked on an urbane smile that missed by a mile. He dry-washed his hands, lifted his eyebrows politely as Liddell stopped.

"I'm Liddell. A boy registered me in this afternoon."

The clerk consulted the register nearsightedly, nodded. "You're in three-fifteen, Mr. Liddell."

"Any messages for me?"

The clerk felt in the pigeonhole numbered 315, turned, managed to look very sad, and shook his head. "No messages."

Liddell nodded, walked down to the iron-grille elevator at the far end of the lobby, and rode to the third floor.

Once in his room, he removed the glass from his handkerchief, breathed on the glass, and held it up to the light. He grunted with satisfaction at the prints that showed up. From his valise he took a roll of transparent

35

tape, a bottle of black powder, and three strips of celluloid.

He dusted the glass with the black powder, examined the prints that showed up critically, and selected the best three. Then, holding the transparent tape taut, he pressed it down over one of the powdered fingerprints. He lifted the tape cautiously, cut it near the roll, transferred it to one of the celluloid strips. He took it to the window, examined the lifted fingerprint, and was satisfied. He repeated the process with two other prints, then replaced powder, tape, and the celluloid strips in his valise.

Back at the table, he picked up the glass and was about to rewrap it in his handkerchief when he heard a slight noise outside his window. He swung around and dropped to one knee.

Behind the curtain, he could make out the dim outline of a man's figure. There was a smash of glass, then two shots that came so close together they sounded like one. Liddell could see them chew bits out of the table near his head. He dove behind the dresser, reached for the bottom drawer where he'd parked his .45, and dragged it out.

Liddell hugged the dresser for a moment, then stuck a cautious eye around the side. The man on the balcony threw two more shots and two holes appeared in the wall over Liddell's head as if by magic. He pulled back, blasted the only light fixture in the room off the wall, throwing the room into darkness.

Then snaking his arm around the dresser, he squeezed the trigger twice and winced at the heavy roar of the .45. Somewhere a woman screamed in shrill French; there was the pounding of running feet. There was no return fire from outside the window.

36

Liddell waited for a ten-second count, crept from behind the dresser, flattened himself on the floor. There was no sign of anybody on the balcony. Cautiously, .45 shoved out in front of him, finger taut on the trigger, he inched toward the window.

The balcony was empty. Liddell threw up the sash, leaned out. Through the ornamental grillwork, he caught sight of a figure with its leg thrown over the far end balcony. He fired at him, the slug screamed wildly as it ricocheted off the metal of the grille.

The man with the gun swung around the last fan-shaped guard screen and reached the end of the balcony. He raised his hand. There was a vicious spit; his hand seemed to belch orange flame. It spat twice more. Once it gouged a piece of concrete from the wall close enough to Liddell's head to sting him with the splinters.

He pulled his head in, rushed for the door, flung it open, and slammed into a big man coming in. The man dug the muzzle of a .38 into Liddell's mid-section. "All right, Jesse James. Drop the artillery," he ordered.

"Get out of my way, I'm—"

The man's voice was hard, low. "Drop it or I'll drop you."

Liddell shrugged, dropped the .45, watched the big man kick it into the darkness of the room. "He's going to get away," he growled.

"Maybe. But you're not. Inside." He slid his hand along the wall until he encountered the overhead switch, flicked it. Nothing happened.

"I had to blast it," Liddell told him. "I was a sitting duck in a lighted room."

"There's a lamp on the dresser. Try it—but don't try anything else," the big man told him. "You won't be a sitting duck—you'll be a dead duck if you do."

37

Liddell walked over to the dresser and snapped on the lamp, spilling a yellow light into the room. Outside in the corridor, heads started to pop cautiously from half-open doors, ready to be jerked back if the shooting started again. At the far end of the hall, some of the hardier souls came out of their rooms and huddled in groups, staring down to where the big man kept his gun trained.

The man with the gun stared around Liddell's wrecked room, whistled. "Been having quite a ball. Fireworks and all. A little early for the Mardi Gras, isn't it?"

"You the house dick?" Liddell wanted to know.

"That's me, McGinnis. Who're you?"

"Liddell. Look, Mac, do you have to hold that gun on me? It makes me nervous looking into that end of a heater."

"Lucky thing for you it's you that's nervous, not me. When I get nervous, I start shooting."

"You'd be making a big mistake. This is my room—"

"If I make a mistake, I'll apologize. You usually go around with a gun in your fist?"

Liddell grunted. "I'm a private detective. I'm down here on a case."

The house man nodded amiably. "Been doing some target practice, no doubt?"

"I didn't shoot the room up," Liddell told him patiently. "Some guy out on the balcony tried to pot me. I got to the window just as he hit the end of the balcony. I thought I could head him off if I got to the stairs fast enough."

Down the hall, the elevator clanged to a stop. The doors slammed open, and the desk clerk bustled up the corridor, face white. "What's going on up here, Mac?" he asked the house detective.

38

The house man didn't take his eyes off Liddell. "Know this guy?"

The clerk peered around the big man's shoulder, saw Liddell, and nodded. "He's a guest. This is his room." He started dry-washing his hands agitatedly. "I'm terribly sorry about this, Mr. Liddell. Mac didn't know you. He—"

McGinnis shrugged and stuck his .38 back in its holster. "Sorry, mister," he told Liddell. "Can't take any chances, you know."

"What happened, Mr. Liddell?" The room clerk turned watery eyes on the private detective.

"Man says somebody tried to blast him from the balcony," McGinnis told him. "Guy got away."

Liddell nodded glumly. "You're sure I didn't have any calls or visitors, eh?" he asked the night clerk.

The clerk coughed nervously and wet his lips with the tip of his tongue. His eyes hopscotched around the room, avoiding Liddell's gaze. "A call did come in for you just after you got back. They said not to bother you —they just wanted your room number. They were going to send something over." The motion of his hands became more agitated. "I thought nothing of it, so I gave them your number."

"And they damn near gave it to me."

There was a brief commotion in the hallway as two men pushed their way through the curious group that had gathered near the doorway. One of the newcomers was in uniform, the other in plain clothes.

"All right, folks. Nothing to see in here. Get back to your rooms," the man in plain clothes told them. He shoved his western sheriff-type hat on the back of his head, nodded to the uniformed man. "Break it up, Ed. Get the hallway cleared."

He stepped into the room, closing the door behind him. He nodded to the house detective and turned to Liddell. "I'm Hennessy. Detective sergeant." His eyes roamed around the room, noted the bullet-scarred dresser, the smashed window. "Looks like you've been having some trouble." He whipped a leather notebook from his pocket. "Let's hear about it."

"Sneak thief, sarge," the house man told him. "Mr. Liddell here apparently walked in on him. He threw a couple of shots, went out the window, ran along the balcony, and got away."

The plain-clothes man grunted, walked over to where Liddell's .45 lay against the wall, picked it up in a handkerchief, and held the barrel to his nose. "This yours?" he asked Liddell.

Liddell nodded.

"Pretty heavy iron to be packing," he commented. "Must have been expecting trouble?"

"I always carry it. It's licensed. I operate a private agency in New York."

The sergeant raised his eyebrows. "Oh, a big-town op, eh? Got anything that says so?"

Liddell reached into his pockets, brought out his credentials, and handed them over. The plain-clothes man riffled through them, copied some information into his notebook, handed the papers back. "You check in at headquarters?"

Liddell shook his head. "Just got in this afternoon. Didn't have time."

The sergeant considered it, shook his head. "You've been in long enough to make somebody mad."

"It was a sneak thief."

The plain-clothes man snapped his notebook with a scowl. "Look, Liddell, maybe I'm only a small-town boy, but don't get cute with me." He jabbed in the direction of the window with his pencil. "The glass is on the floor inside the room. That means it was broken by somebody outside. Somebody who was waiting for you."

Liddell shrugged. "It doesn't figure. I've only been in town a few hours."

Hennessy stuck the notebook back in his hip pocket. "Don't mean a thing. Don't take some guys as long as others to get unpopular. Some guys got a knack for it." He dropped Liddell's .45 into his jacket pocket. "Suppose we take a run downtown and have a talk."

"What about?"

The plain-clothes man shrugged. "We're the curious kind. We like to know who's buzzing our territory."

"I'm very sorry about all this, Mr. Liddell." The room clerk looked on the verge of crying. "Is there anything I can do?"

Liddell jammed his hat on the back of his head. "Yeah, when I come back from the Bastille, have my stuff moved to another room. One that doesn't front on the municipal firing range."

5.

JOHNNY LIDDELL squirmed on the hard wooden chair in City Hall. His watch showed the time to be 1:10. He lit his fourth cigarette in a half hour from the butt of the last one, swearing under his breath.

He glared at a frosted glass door that stated "District Attorney—Private" in gleaming gold leaf. Finally he got up from the chair and walked over to a railing-enclosed space where a male stenographer was typing out a deposition.

"How long they figuring on keeping me here? I've had a bad day," he complained.

The male stenographer looked up, scowled at him. "Look, it's like the story of the Chinaman and the two guys to hold him. I don't like it, either. I don't get no double time for overtime. Go on over and sit down. When they want you, they'll call you." He went back to his typing.

The intercom on the stenographer's desk buzzed. He flipped a button. "Yes, sir?"

The intercom chattered back at him. He nodded, flipped the button to off.

"They want you now." He nodded toward the glass door. "And if you've had a bad day, mister, from the way the boss sounds, the night's not going to be exactly a breeze either."

Liddell dropped his cigarette to the floor and ground it out. He walked over and entered the room, closing the door behind him. Hennessy, the detective sergeant, lounged comfortably in a wooden armchair across the desk from a tall thin man in a loose-fitting tweed jacket.

"I'm Wilson, the district attorney." The man behind the desk pasted a smile on his thin lips but made no effort to get up. "I'm sorry if you've had to wait." His tone didn't bear out the words. "You know Sergeant Hennessy?"

Liddell nodded. "I wouldn't exactly say we've struck up an undying friendship, but we've met."

Wilson nodded. He touched the tips of his fingers together, studied Liddell. "The sergeant thought we should meet. So there would be no future misunderstandings. You understand?" He smiled again, but it consisted merely of a twisting upward of the corners of his mouth. The cold expression in his eyes was unchanged. "Won't you sit down?"

Liddell crossed the room and dropped into an armchair facing the desk. "I don't know what this is all about, Mr. Wilson. An attempt was made on my life. I fired back in self-defense. I have a license for my gun."

The district attorney nodded. He was tall, loose-jointed. He wore his hair long, parted low on the left side, little kinky curls over his right ear. His nose was broad at the base, inclined to a slight hook, his dark face hinting at traces of mixed blood generations back. "No one questions your right to defend yourself. The only question that does occur to me is why it would be necessary." He held his well-manicured hands out, palms up. "You're a stranger in town. We're concerned."

43

Liddell nodded. "I'll bet." He pulled a pack of cigarettes from his pocket. "O.K.?"

The sergeant shifted in his chair. "Look, Liddell, don't give us that persecuted act. This is no third degree." He reached over to the edge of the desk, picked up a card. "The Benton Agency registered you yesterday as an op. You didn't get here until today. You're not here twenty-four hours when there's gunplay. We want to know why."

"Maybe I looked like rich pickings for a sneak thief. He was giving my stuff a going over when—"

"In the Delcort? Rich pickings? The only thing you could pick up in that flea bag couldn't be sold on the open market. It might be traded, but—"

Wilson cut him off with a gesture from a well-manicured hand. "I think we'll get further if we stop underestimating each other's intelligence, sergeant." He leaned back and refolded his hands across his chest. "Certainly, Liddell, you don't expect us to believe that a sneak thief attempted to rob you, closed the window, then shot through it?"

Liddell smoked silently, offering no comment.

"By the same token, we don't expect you to believe that every time somebody defends himself against felonious assault in New Orleans, I come to my office for a midnight conference on it."

"What do you want me to tell you?"

The district attorney leaned forward. "Who that man was on the balcony and why he tried to kill you."

Liddell sighed. "I went all over that with the sergeant."

"Suppose you go all over it again with me?" There was a hard note in the district attorney's suave tones.

"Well, I came back from a date—"

44

"With?"

"Gabby Benton."

The sergeant snorted. "His boss," he told the D.A. "Naturally, she'd back him up on anything."

"When I walked into my room," Liddell ignored the interruption, "I thought I noticed something or someone on my balcony. The glass broke, and he started throwing lead. I ducked behind the bureau, fished my gun from the bottom drawer, shot back at him."

A quick flash of annoyance wiped the last vestiges of simulated good nature from the district attorney's face. "You haven't told us who the man was or why he was there, Liddell." He snapped up the cover of a humidor, selected a fat Havana, bit the end off it, spat it at a square leather wastebasket. "Suppose we come to that part?"

"I don't know who he was," Liddell told him flatly.

"What are you doing in New Orleans?" Hennessy shot at him.

"I was brought in on a case that Gabby Benton was afraid was getting too big to handle alone."

"What case?"

Liddell considered, then decided to play it straight. "A man disappeared. A man named Brother Alfred. We're trying to find him."

Wilson rolled the unlit cigar in the center of his mouth and fixed the private detective with the cold glare of his eyes.

"That happened in another parish. That has nothing to do with the city."

Liddell shrugged. "You know that. Now I know it. But maybe the guy who tried to get me doesn't know it."

"Possibly you consider this episode amusing," the

45

district attorney told him. "I don't. We will not stand for out-of-town gangsters or," he shrugged, "private detectives using this town as a dueling ground. That went out a hundred years ago. This town is law abiding, and we intend to keep it that way."

Liddell nodded. "Suits me. Having guys use my hide as a private shooting gallery isn't exactly my idea of fun, either." He leaned over, crushed his cigarette out in a metal ash tray on the corner of the desk. "Can I go now?"

Wilson studied him coldly. "You're free to go any time you wish, Liddell. We have no charges against you—yet."

"My gun?" he asked Hennessy.

The sergeant looked to the district attorney quizzically.

"We understand each other, Liddell?" the district attorney asked. "There is to be no shooting, no gunplay."

"I've got a license for the gun."

"Exactly. You have a license for the gun. That does not give you the license to use it indiscriminately." He flicked his eyes from Liddell to the sergeant. "Give him his gun, sergeant."

Hennessy nodded. "It'll be up any minute."

Liddell scowled. "You had it with you."

"That's right," the sergeant nodded. "But I sent it down to ballistics. We want a couple of slugs on file. It'll make it a lot easier to keep tabs on you." He chewed on the end of his thumbnail, staring at Liddell morosely. "I don't have to remind you that the only permit issued is for that particular .45?"

Liddell didn't answer, returned his stare.

"If you have any other guns with you, I'd advise you to turn them in. Because if we catch you with an unlicensed gun in your possession, Liddell, I'm personally going to toss you into the calaboz and throw away the key."

The clerk at the Delcort waved Johnny Liddell down excitedly as he came in the lobby. Liddell stopped by the desk on his way to the elevators.

"Is everything all right, Mr. Liddell?" he wanted to know anxiously.

"Just peachy dandy. Look, just let me get some sleep. I'll give you all the details some other time." He held out his hand. "What room did you move me to?"

"Room three-forty. You won't need a key. Miss Benton is up there."

"What do you mean Miss Benton is up there?"

The clerk's hand started to tremble. He steadied it with his other hand, tried a confident grin. It didn't fool even him. "She—she came in about a half hour after you left. Somebody must have told her about the shooting." He cast a baleful glare at the house detective, who was lounging on a chair in the corner reading a newspaper. "She came right over."

"You're sure it's Miss Benton?" Liddell growled.

"Oh, yes. Positive." The clerk's head bobbed like a cork on a stormy sea. "I know Miss Benton for many years. She—uh—"

Liddell nodded. "I know. She uses this place for her setup raids. O.K., as long as you're sure."

Liddell took the elevator to the third floor, followed the corridor to 340. He listened outside the door for a moment, slipped the .45 from its shoulder holster to his right-hand pocket. Then he pushed the door open.

Gabby Benton jumped up from a chair, ran to him. "Where've you been? You've had me worried stiff!" she accused.

47

"Meeting the D.A. and a tough dick named Hennessey." He accepted the invitation in her upturned lips, then tossed his hat at the bed. He walked over to the table, picked up a glass the girl had been drinking out of, smelled it, took a deep swallow.

"What'd Wilson want?" Gabby followed him to the table and stared into his face curiously. "He didn't have anything on you."

Liddell shook his head, added some more liquor to the glass from an open bottle. "He was just reading me the rules of the court. It seems that he intends to bag me, but good. Being a sportsman, he doesn't want to shoot a sitting duck. When he gives me the works, he wants me to know why."

"Did you tell him about Marty Kirk bringing you down?"

Liddell shook his head. "He didn't ask me."

Gabby lifted the glass from his hand, took a drink. "Now suppose you tell me what the hell it was all about?" She walked over and sat on the side of the bed. "All McGinnis told me was that somebody tried to pot you through the window."

Liddell shrugged out of his jacket, loosened the top button of his collar, tugged the tie down. "So that's how you knew? The house dick."

"I throw quite a bit of change his way," Gabby nodded. "Whenever we're setting up a raid, it's nice to have the house dick in your corner. He didn't know you were a friend of mine until he checked your registration card. The boy from the Roosevelt checked you in, put my car registration down. Mac recognized it." She watched Liddell from under half-closed lids. "You still didn't tell me who tried to get you."

"I don't know. He got away. That big flatfoot friend of yours showed up in the doorway just as I went after the guy. He held a gun on me just long enough for the guy on the balcony to get away."

Gabby scowled, bit on the tip of a lacquered nail. "Who could it be?" She watched Liddell intently. "Anything happen out at the temple when you went back?"

"Nothing much. I did get what I went for." He snapped his fingers, went to the drawer, went through each drawer carefully, then swore fervently. Then he went through his valise, looked up. "It's gone."

"No use of you worrying alone. Tell me so I can worry too. What's gone?"

Liddell slammed the drawers closed, walked back to the table, and poured himself another drink. "Alfred's glass." He tossed the drink off and grimaced. "It had his fingerprints all over it. I picked it up at the temple tonight in his personal washroom."

"And it's gone?" Gabby groaned.

Liddell nodded. "I had it when the shooting started."

Gabby smoothed the wrinkles out of her brow with the tips of her fingers. "Well, that's that. Now you're back looking for a guy with a beard he can shave off, a—"

"Correction, please," Liddell told her wearily. "Alfred doesn't have a beard. I doubt if he ever had one."

"How do you know? You never saw him."

Liddell nodded. "Just the same he doesn't have one. Not unless Wanda shaves. There was a full shaving kit in his closet."

Gabby groaned. "It looks like our chances of qualifying for that five-thousand reward are fading fast." She shook her head. "I would have sworn that was a real beard."

49

"Maybe it was. Maybe he shaved it off just before he disappeared. But I'd bet my share of the money he doesn't have one now."

"And you had his prints," Gabby groaned. "If you'd only dropped the glass off at my place, or stuck it in the safe."

"I didn't have much of a chance to do anything, as you may remember. The police marched in and waltzed me off with them."

"Would it pay to go back there with a fingerprint kit and—"

Liddell shook his head. "How could you isolate prints that belonged to Alfred? Of course, if we could get some prints off that delicious dish he had out there, that Wanda—"

"They'd more likely be Marty Kirk's than Alfred's," Gabby put in.

Liddell stared at her. "Marty's?"

Gabby nodded. "Marty's been crazy about her for years. My guess is that he has her at the temple to keep an eye on Alfred."

"Then there is some kind of a tie-up between Kirk and Alfred?"

Gabby shrugged. "I don't know anything more than that, Johnny. There are a lot of rumors—that Marty supplies the temple with its dope and provides the muscle whenever the temple needs it. But they're only rumors. I couldn't say they were true."

Liddell thought it over, scratched his head. "That might account for Wanda seeming so indifferent about Alfred's being among the missing." He shook his head. "Well, one thing's for sure. We're not going to prove anything by sitting up all night talking about it. You better be on your way home. It's getting late."

50

"On our way home, you mean. You're not going to stay here, are you?" the blonde argued. "Whoever it was might come back."

Liddell grinned, walked over, caught the girl by the elbow, and lifted her to her feet. "Look, baby, I'm more likely to live to a ripe old age if I stay right here." He led her to the door and opened it. "Your hospitality's enough to kill a guy."

She made a face at him. "I suppose you know a better way to die?" She slammed the door after her.

After the blonde left, Liddell walked over to his valise, fumbled in its depths, and brought out the three strips of celluloid on which he'd put Alfred's fingerprints. He took an envelope out of the dresser drawer, scribbled a note, wrapped the celluloid strips in it, and sealed the envelope. He addressed it, affixed a stamp to the corner, walked out into the hall, and dropped it down the mail chute.

6.

THE PEALING of the phone at his ear was shrill, strident, insistent. Johnny Liddell groaned, cursed softly, and dug his head under the pillow. The noise refused to go away. He opened one eye experimentally, squinted at the window shade, and noted that it still wasn't light.

He tried to wipe the sleep from his eyes, but it wouldn't wipe away. The phone kept dancing on the stand. He reached out, snagged the receiver from its hook, jammed it against his ear.

"What's the matter? The joint on fire?" he growled into the receiver.

"Sorry, Mr. Liddell." The operator's metallic voice sounded bored. "Lady said it was a matter of life and death."

Liddell yawned, nodded. "Put her on."

There was a faint click, then the husky voice of Sister Wanda came through. "I'm sorry to have to bother you at this hour, Mr. Liddell. I didn't think the occasion would arise to have to speak to you again. But something has happened." She paused. "I've heard from Brother Alfred."

"Where is he?"

"Hiding."

Liddell scowled. "Why?"

"He believes his life is in danger. He merely called to assure me that he was safe. When I told him about you, he insisted that he see you."

Liddell swung his legs out of bed. "Good. When and where?"

"As soon as possible."

"Now. Where do I find him?"

"He'll find you. Here are your instructions."

"Wait'll I get a pencil." Liddell snapped on the bed light, reached to the back of the chair where his jacket hung, and pulled a pencil and notebook from the inside pocket. "Shoot."

"Do you know how to get to West End Park? It's near the yacht basin."

"Better give me the directions," Liddell told her. "I'm a stranger in town."

"It's very simple. You know how to get to Canal from your hotel?"

Liddell nodded. "Yeah."

"Good. Canal separates old New Orleans from the modern part. The park is in the new section. You will follow Canal Street to the boulevard leading to Pontchartrain. You will come to the Delgado Museum. Exactly three miles farther there is a small dirt road. It's marked dead end. You will drive to the end of it and park with your lights on. Brother Alfred will come to you."

"Don't I need a secret password?" Liddell growled. "Why all the hocus-pocus? Can't he just—"

"The meeting will be on his terms," the receiver told him tartly.

Liddell sighed, squinted at the luminescent face of the clock on his stand. "It's two thirty now. I can't be there much before four."

"He will be waiting." There was a click as the connection was broken.

Liddell dropped the receiver back on its hook and scowled at it. He reached for a cigarette on his night stand, stuck it in the corner of his mouth, and touched a light to it.

On an impulse, he reached over, lifted the receiver from the hook, gave the operator the number Marty Kirk had given him. There was a brief pause, then the heavy, throaty voice of the racketeer came through.

"Yeah?"

"This is Liddell. I've got news for you."

The man at the other end snorted. "It better be good."

"I'm meeting your boy at four."

The voice on the other end sounded impressed. "How'd you reach him?"

"That's a professional secret. I just wanted to tell you to get that five gees ready for a pickup."

"You deliver the merchandise, we'll have your payoff."

Liddell nodded. "O.K. Set your alarm, because I expect to have him back at that hocus-pocus joint of his in time for breakfast." He dropped the receiver back on its cradle, grinned at it. Then he snubbed his cigarette out and called down to the desk for a hired car. He told them to have it waiting in a half hour.

A miserable, cold drizzle had started by the time Johnny Liddell was ready to leave. He picked up the rented sedan in front of the Delcort, drove down Bourbon Street, swung into Canal. Most of the store fronts and windows were blank, dark, as Liddell tooled the rented car along the broad street. He passed the stately Boston Club, where the Mardi Gras King greets his

54

Queen on Mardi Gras day, and headed uptown away from the river toward the lake.

As he drove past the famous light stanchions, each decorated with the four flags that have flown over the city in its turbulent history, the character of the neighborhood slowly changed. The business district, the colorful Vieux Carré, fell far behind.

He drove into a district of big estates, their gardens abloom with roses and fragrantes. The houses themselves were huge, white, porticoed ghosts set back from the road, half hidden by giant moss-bearing oaks, so old and freighted with memories of centuries that their branches trailed the ground. Soon the estates, too, fell behind. He swung into the City Park, with its famous dueling oaks and the ghosts of thousands of gallants who'd lost their lives under them.

About forty minutes from his hotel, he came into sight of the Greek temple known as the Delgado Museum. He cut his speed and checked his speedometer. Three miles beyond the museum, he came upon the little dirt road with a weather-beaten sign that proclaimed it to be a dead end.

He swung the rented car off the macadam and fitted his wheels into a rutted track that led back through a clump of trees. The car bumped its way along a road that was barely wide enough for one car's passage. After a mile or more of jouncing, he came to what was apparently the end of the road, a little promontory set high above the scenic highway, completely surrounded by trees and dense underbrush. He braked the car to a stop and looked around.

There was no sign of life of any kind.

Liddell tugged his .45 from its holster and put it on

the car seat beside him. He opened the car door and walked to the end of the road in the chilling drizzle. It consisted of a couple of logs piled into a barrier. Beyond, the land fell away for several hundred feet of boulder-spiked hillside. On either side of the road, the ground rose to wooded wilderness. Far out he could hear the occasional hoot of a lake boat feeling its way through the mist.

He walked back to the car, brought out the pint he had stuck in the glove compartment, held it to his lips, and tilted it. The brandy helped take some of the chill out of his bones.

One moment he was alone, straining eyes and ears against the wall of darkness. The next there was a figure standing beside the car. It was that of a fairly short man dressed eerily in a white robe that stirred restlessly in the breeze. The lower part of his face was covered by a bushy black beard, he wore heavy horn-rimmed glasses, and his head gleamed baldly in the half-light.

"You are Johnny Liddell?" His voice was deep, theatrically rumbling. It was the kind of voice that would have a carefully calculated effect on an emotional audience.

Liddell started. His hand sought the .45 on the seat beside him and closed about the reassuringly cold metal of its butt.

"I am Alfred," the voice continued. From its tone, it was apparent that the listener was supposed to drop to his knees. Liddell had no difficulty resisting the impulse. "I have been told that you seek to help."

Liddell relaxed, let the air out of his lungs with a slow whistle. "Don't sneak up on a guy like that, mister," he advised. "Not in these surroundings." He pulled out his pint, helped himself to a deep slug, offered it through the window. "Take the chill off?"

The bearded man shook his head. "Alcohol is against my teaching. You wish to talk? Come, I will lead you to my retreat."

"Can't we drive there?"

The man turned on his heel and started away. Liddell reluctantly pushed open the car door and followed him. "Near here?"

"You will soon see," the bearded man boomed. "Perhaps you think these precautions silly. But you must understand that there are those who would destroy me because I am dedicated to drive them from their citadels of Sin. Nothing must happen to me until I have finished my work."

"Nothing's going to happen to you. Marty Kirk and his boys have more to lose by your death than by your living. I'm here to guarantee you safe conduct back to your temple."

The bearded man shook his head sadly. "You would take the word of a creature of Mammon? Do you not see that—" There was a sudden convulsion of his features. He crooked up a protective arm in front of his face.

Liddell started to swing around, heard rather than saw the blow that dropped him. There was a hissing rush of sound from behind. He tried to spin, to fall away from what was coming. It hummed like a bumblebee and exploded on the side of his head with a brilliance of a flare. He tried to tug the .45 from his pocket, but suddenly it had become too heavy. It slipped from his limp fingers and clattered to the ground.

There was another swish, another display of fireworks in the back of his skull, and he went to his knees. He tried to pull himself to his feet, but his knees had turned to jelly. He pitched forward on his face and didn't move.

It was the penetrating cold, the persistent call of some wood bird that convinced Johnny Liddell that he was still alive. His head swirled sickeningly, and the call of the bird echoed back and forth in diminishing volume with a monotony that grated on his nerves.

He struggled to get his eyes open, but a black pit from which he was trying to climb yawned again. When he moved his head, nausea enveloped him, and he slid back into the void. He tried to cry out as the sinking sensation assailed him, but it came out of his throat as no more than a hollow groan.

After awhile, the dark void receded. A pain that started behind his ear exploded in a bright flash. His eyes felt as though they were leaded down and stubbornly resisted his efforts to open them. Finally, when he did get them open, he had difficulty keeping them from rolling back in his head.

There was sky and a tree branch over his head. He managed to sit up, look around. The car stood where he had left it. The sky had lightened with the coming of day, transforming the drizzle of the night before into a damp fog that lay in the hollows around him like an opaque cloud. He crawled back to his car on hands and knees, managed to get the door open. The bottle was still on the seat where he had left it the night before.

He tilted the brandy over his lips, took a long swig. Another wave of giddiness assailed him, then passed. He still had the pain behind his eyes, but the mists in front of them were fast dissipating.

The man in the white robe was nowhere to be seen.

After a moment, Liddell was able to get out of the car, look around. There were signs of a struggle. Mashed into the ground near the front of the car were the remains of a pair of horn-rimmed spectacles, the rims smashed, the lenses shattered. He picked them up and dropped them into his jacket pocket. His .45 lay where he had dropped it. He checked it, found it untouched, and replaced it in its shoulder holster.

Liddell cursed under his breath and pulled up his jacket collar in an abortive effort to keep out the chill that was beginning to numb his fingers and his feet. He tried to burn it out with another slug from the bottle but decided his wet clothes had too much of an edge.

He got back into the car, kicked it into roaring life, managed to get it turned around in the narrow clearing. He showed less concern for the car's springs on the way back over the rutted road, roaring along it like a drunken panzer tank.

He headed back past the golf course and found a phone in a small coffee and doughnut shop on the boulevard. He put through a call to Marty Kirk at his penthouse. The number failed to answer. Liddell slammed the receiver back on its hook, cursing bitterly.

He had two cups of coffee so hot they almost scalded him, and got back into the car. He headed for his hotel and some dry clothes.

He was under a shower when the knock came at his door. He ignored it, finished showering, and rubbed himself down with a heavy Turkish towel. He got into a dry pair of shorts and walked out into his bedroom.

Hook, the little man with the thick black hair, whom he'd first met in New York, looked up and grinned. "Hello, Liddell. Long time no see."

Liddell scowled at him, walked over, examined the lock. "A helluva lot of privacy they give you in this rat trap. First they use my room for a shooting gallery, now they've routed traffic through it. How'd you get in here?"

The little man looked hurt. "You wouldn't figure that lock would give me any trouble, would you? I could get that one open by blowing on it."

"What do you want?"

"Same as always. The boss wants to see you."

Liddell grinned at him glumly. "I got news for you, little man. I want to see your boss, too." He stuffed his legs into his pants. "I called him an hour or so ago. Where was he?"

"He didn't say."

Liddell nodded. "There are a lot of things he didn't say. Maybe this time he's going to be more talkative." He yanked out a drawer, pulled a shirt out. "I don't like playing with a stacked deck."

Hook sighed. "If I was you, I wouldn't go looking for any grief, shamus. I got the feeling the boss isn't too happy with you right now."

"That spoils my whole day. You know what? I'm not very happy with you or your boss or this stinking town." He knotted a tie around his neck, shrugged into his jacket. "Where's your boss now?"

"Waiting for you."

"Well, we mustn't keep Marty waiting." He took a snub-nosed .38 from his top drawer, dropped it into his jacket pocket. "Let's go have a talk with the little man."

Marty Kirk lived in the swank Carter Arms, an expensive pile of stone and plate glass that towered over Lafayette Square. The lobby was furnished in aggressively modernistic style. Brightly colored couches and chrome tables tastefully complemented the soft, restful, ankle-deep pastel carpeting. Hook led the way across the lobby to an ornate registration desk where an impeccably dressed man was engaged in the absorbing task of adjusting the edge of a cuff that peeked from the end of the sleeve of his morning jacket.

"Ring the penthouse and tell Mr. Kirk that Liddell and me are on our way up, will you?"

The clerk raised his eyes, nodded. "Of course." His fingers played with the ends of a linen handkerchief tucked in his breast pocket.

A man sitting on one of the couches yawned, put his paper down. He got up, strolled across the lobby.

Hook led the way past a bank of elevators to one marked "Penthouse." The tired-looking man who had been reading the paper on the couch stepped into the cage behind them and nodded for the operator to take it up.

"He clean, Hook?" the tired man wanted to know.

"Packing a peashooter, Tim." Hook turned to Liddell. "Tim here runs the checkroom for the boss. You check your hardware with him on the way in on account of the boss is very nervous about guns. Especially when someone else has them."

The tall, tired-looking man leaned against the elevator wall, held out his hand. He made no effort to wipe the boredom from his eyes. "You won't need a check. I'll remember you."

Liddell grinned, pulled the .38 from his pocket, and passed it over. "Take good care of it. I may be needing it."

Tim nodded, hefted the .38 in his palm, looked it over incuriously. "Nice iron." He dropped it into his jacket pocket. "You'll get it back. One way or another."

The elevator glided to a smooth stop at the penthouse, and the doors slid noiselessly open. A man sat at a small desk, paring his nails with a gold pocketknife. He looked Liddell over from head to foot. "He all set to see the boss?"

Tim nodded, brought the .38 from his pocket. "Now he is." He dropped the gun back into his pocket.

"You better cover the desk here, Hook. I'll take care of him." He nodded for Liddell to follow him and knocked three times on a metal door. There was the stuttering of a buzzer, and the door swung open.

Marty Kirk stood in the center of the room, a glass in his hand. He scowled at Liddell as the private detective walked in.

"Well, where's the hallelujah shouter? You said you'd deliver him this morning." He snapped his wrist up, flicked back his sleeve, glared at the gold watch on his wrist. "It's after ten."

Liddell studied the gang boss, scowled. He got the impression Marty Kirk was scared. There was a fine film of perspiration on his forehead and his upper lip. The hand shook as he lifted the glass to his mouth, drained it. "Well, where is he?"

"You ought to know where Alfred is, Kirk," Liddell snapped back.

Kirk nodded. "You're damn right I do. And no thanks to you." He raised a clenched fist, brought it down on the arm of his chair. "What was the idea of the snow job over the phone? You said you were going to see him."

"I did see him."

Kirk snorted. "You're a liar. You said you were going to meet him out at the lake. He was nowhere near the lake. He's been hiding out over in San Vincente all the time." He pointed a finger at Liddell. "You didn't know that he was taking a powder, did you?"

"Look, Kirk, I've had a bad night and I've got bumps

to prove it. Alfred was nowhere near San Vincente when I saw him. If he got there, someone took him there."

"You saw him?"

Liddell nodded violently. "You're damn right I saw him."

"Then why didn't you bring him in like you said you would?" Kirk's eyes narrowed. They were inflamed, red-rimmed. He was having difficulty controlling a little twitch under his left eye. "How come?"

"Because I was sapped, that's how come. But I'll find him again. And when I do turn him up—"

"The only way you'll turn him up now is with a spade. He's dead."

Liddell blinked. "Dead?"

Kirk picked up a bottle by the neck and tilted it over his glass. "If he's not, they're fixing to play him a dirty trick. They're going to bury him tomorrow."

The vein in the center of Liddell's forehead grew prominent, throbbed. He grabbed Kirk by the front of his coat and pulled him close. "So you crossed me! You used me to bird-dog him for you, then you killed him!"

"Get your hands off the boss." Kirk's bodyguard's voice was low, loaded with menace.

Liddell pushed Kirk away from him. "That was a sucker play, Marty. Nobody uses me as a finger for a hit." His voice was ice cold, low. "I'm going to pin it right around your neck."

"Should I throw him out, boss?" The man from the outside office stood, hand sunk in jacket pocket, a tell-tale bulge in his fist.

"I'm not finished with him, Leo. When I'm finished, you can throw him out." Kirk finished his drink, slammed the glass down. He spun on Liddell. "And they told me you were smart. You think I'd stick my neck out?" He wiped the wet smear of his lips with the back of his hand, had to steady himself on the corner of the desk. "He killed himself."

"You won't sell that package, Kirk. Not while I'm around."

"Maybe you're not going to be around long, shamus," the bodyguard put in.

Liddell ignored the interruption. "I was with him at four this morning. He had no intention of killing himself then, and—"

"So he didn't figure on dying. Accidents happen."

"What kind of accident?"

"Piled his car into a tree. Burned all to hell and gone, him and the car. Musta had a snoot full of liquor."

Liddell snorted. "His sect didn't believe in liquor."

Kirk grinned loosely. "It's like I always say. You can't trust nobody these days." He wagged a finger under Liddell's nose drunkenly. "My friend the sheriff of San Vincente says car and Alfred all soaked with liquor." He shook his head. "Sad way to go."

"I'm not buying it, Kirk."

"Give him his money and get him out of here. See he leaves town, Leo."

"Keep your money. I don't sell out. I warned you I wouldn't stand still for it if anything happened to him when I turned him up. It still goes."

The bodyguard grinned at him. The grin never made his eyes. "You don't catch on very fast, sucker. Accidents can happen to anybody. The hallelujah shouter. You. Anybody."

"Maybe so. You remember something, too. A lot of people can get hurt in an accident on its way to happen. Somebody took a potshot at me last night. If I happen

64

to trace it to this end of town, I'll be looking you up."

"Do that," Leo told him. "Only when you're looking at me, be sure you can see. There are a lot of guys who came looking for me—only they couldn't see me. It happens that way sometimes."

Kirk cut him off with a wave of his hand. "Cut it out, both of you. You're scaring me to death." He focused his eyes on Liddell with difficulty. "I told you I'd pay you off. What do you want to hang around for? Your job's finished."

"Finished? Hell, Kirk, it's just begun!"

7.

JOHNNY LIDDELL took the elevator down to the lobby of Marty Kirk's apartment building, asked the starter where the telephones were. He was directed to a bank of phones at the rear of the lobby and ambled back, paying no attention to the lazy-eyed lobby guide who'd ridden down in the elevator with him.

He dropped a coin in the box and dialed Gabby Benton's office.

"No wonder you didn't want to come back with me," she snapped at him. "You sure didn't stay in that room of yours very long."

"The house dick again, eh? I see where Mr. McGinnis and I have an overdue talk coming."

"Where'd you go at four in the morning that you had to hire a car? I could've driven you any place you wanted to go."

Liddell grunted. "I got a sudden overwhelming yen for fresh air. I went out toward the lake and slept in the City Park all night."

"It was pouring all morning."

"No wonder I got so wet," he growled. "Look, baby, I didn't call you to get a third degree. I don't feel like answering questions from anybody. I've had a bad twenty-four hours."

A note of concern crept into Gabby's voice. "Something happen?"

"Something happen, she says?" Liddell groaned. "No. Just that our friend Brother Alfred is no longer with us."

The gasp came over the wire. "When?"

"A couple of hours ago. I can't talk here. Want to meet me someplace and I'll fill you in?"

"Where are you now?"

"Kirk's place. Off Lafayette Square on Charles."

Gabby hesitated. "How about the French Market? Nobody can get close enough to listen in. And you know how to get there."

Liddell considered it, nodded. "Sounds O.K. to me. Leave now. I'll get there as fast as I can."

Gabby Benton was on her second cup of coffee, third cigarette, and fourth fingernail when Johnny Liddell stepped out of a cab at the curb. She had selected a sidewalk table well separated from the rest of the patrons. Liddell looked around, nodded his approval, slid into a chair opposite her.

"What'd you do, take the fifty-cent tour through the Vieux Carré?" Gabby complained. "I could have gotten here faster than that on my hands and knees."

Liddell looked at the coffee-stained menu, put it aside, flagged a waitress down. He ordered a large cup of black coffee, a double order of doughnuts. As soon as the waitress was out of earshot, Gabby leaned forward.

"Alfred's dead? You're sure?"

Liddell nodded. "They've got him in the morgue over in San Vincente Parish."

"How did it happen?"

Liddell shrugged. "It's supposed to be an accident.

67

Alfred was driving with a skinful of hooch, piled the heap into a tree, and the car burned to a cinder."

The blonde chewed on the inside of her cheek, studied Liddell with narrowed eyes. "But you don't believe it?" she demanded.

Liddell shook his head.

"Why not?" Gabby argued. "You saw what goes at the temple. All that holier than thou stuff is just a pose."

Liddell leaned back and waited until the waitress had deposited a large mug of coffee and a plate piled high with hot doughnuts. She added a glass of water, pattered off.

"I know he wasn't driving the car. He was with me at four thirty this morning in the City Park. If I'm any judge, he had a good jolt of dope in him when I met him. Rum and that kind of coke don't mix."

"You were with him? Why didn't you bring him in? Then we could pack this whole thing in and—"

"I was sapped. I told you I slept in the City Park all night. I must have been out two to three hours." He touched the still tender spot behind his ear. "When I came to, he was gone."

"Maybe he got away and was running away from whoever conked you—"

"Without these?" He dug into his jacket pocket and pulled out the smashed spectacles. He laid them down beside her cup. "Take a look at the thickness of that lens."

Gabby picked it up, rotated it in front of her eye. "Pretty strong correction."

"He couldn't have driven a foot in the daylight without these. Let alone at night."

"Where'd you get them?"

"They were laying on the ground when I came to. They were all mashed into the mud as if there'd been a hell of a struggle."

"What's it mean?"

Liddell scowled. "It means he was murdered. That accident is as phony as a three-dollar bill."

"You think Kirk was behind it?"

"Who else?"

Gabby worried her fingernail between her teeth. "How could he? If he knew where Alfred was, he didn't need to bring you all the way—"

Liddell snorted. "He didn't know. He needed somebody to turn up Alfred. Like a damn fool, I called Kirk to tell him I was going to meet Alfred. He must have had one of his goons follow me, conk me, and set up the phony accident."

"What are you going to do about it?"

"I'm going to prove it was murder and hang it right around Kirk's neck." Liddell tasted his coffee, burned his tongue, swore under his breath. "There's only one catch."

"What's that?"

"The accident happened in San Vincente Parish. Kirk owns the sheriff and the whole shooting match lock, stock, and barrel."

Gabby nodded. "That's for sure." She dumped a fresh cigarette from the pack on the table, lit it from a butt in front of Liddell. "That's not going to make it any easier."

"Unless—"

"Unless what?"

Liddell jabbed his index finger in her direction. "Unless you come up with somebody heavy enough to off-set Kirk's influence over there."

Gabby shook her head sadly. "There ain't no such animal. The sheriff is top man, and—"

"Maybe we can find somebody who can keep the sheriff from throwing his weight around."

"You got a for instance?"

"A newspaper. A good loud one, the louder the better."

"What do they get out of bucking the parish machine?"

Liddell shrugged. "An exclusive."

Gabby plucked at her lower lip with thumb and forefinger. "The *Dispatch* might play ball. They've got nothing to lose."

"The *Dispatch?*"

"A new tab," Gabby told him. "Started up a couple of years ago. Goes in heavily for sensational stuff—murders, rapes. You know the kind."

"Got a contact up there?"

Gabby nodded. "Larry Dunlop. He used to be with the *Item*. He—" She broke off. "You should remember Larry. He was doing a column for the *Item* when you were here right after the war."

Liddell ridged his forehead. "He did the 'Our Town' column? A skinny redheaded guy? Used to practically live at Arnaud's?"

"That's the guy. He left the *Item* when this new sheet started. He's running the whole show now."

"Can you reach him?"

Gabby checked her watch against the big clock on the terminal across the way. "The *Dispatch* is a morning sheet and it's only eleven. He doesn't usually show until about three."

"Can't you reach him at home?" Liddell persisted.

Gabby dug into her handbag, came up with a leather-covered notebook, flipped through the pages. "I've got a number here. I don't know if he'll be at it."

"Try him, will you, Gabby? Tell him I want to meet him. Any place he says."

She pushed back her chair, got up. "Shall I tell him what it's about?"

"Just tell him I'm willing to shove a first-class exclusive his way if he'll back my play."

Gabby nodded, then walked across the court to the building where a telephone booth could be seen through the window. The sheathlike skirt she wore emphasized the shapeliness of her hips and thighs as she walked.

The coffee and doughnuts succeeded in improving Johnny Liddell's outlook on life. He leaned back and enjoyed the shadows, the coolness of the morning. Down Royal Street he could see the spire of Cathedral St. Louis reaching up into the late morning mists, standing its eternal guard over Jackson Square. Across the street the long rows of squat houses, with their uniform iron balconies, stretched for blocks.

He was finishing his second cup of coffee when Gabby returned.

"O.K.?" he asked as she slid into her chair.

"He's coming downtown to his office." She checked her watch again. "He said he'd be there in about twenty minutes."

"Did he go for it?"

Gabby shrugged. "He'll listen."

Liddell nodded. "That's all I need. Does his sheet pack much weight in town?"

"I don't know how much weight it packs, but it makes enough noise." She passed over a pink-colored tabloid. "I picked up a copy at the stand over there. You

71

made the third page." She flipped it open to a two-column head:

"SHOOTING SCRAPE IN QUARTER;
NEW YORK EYE IS INVOLVED"

The story ran for almost half a column.

Liddell ran his eye over it, grunted. "I don't have to read about it. I was there." He flipped through the rest of the pages and nodded. "This is just the kind of rag I had in mind."

"I won't be able to go along with you to Dunlop's office, Johnny. I've got a twelve-thirty date back at my shop. If you think it's important that I go along, I may be able to postpone—"

Liddell rolled up the *Dispatch* and stuck it under his chair. "Keep your appointment. There's nothing you can do on this deal. Either Dunlop goes for my pitch or he doesn't. If he doesn't, there's no need for you to be there, and if he does you've already done your share."

Gabby nodded. "O.K., then I won't come along. When am I going to see you?"

"Dinner tonight?"

The blonde shook her head. "We're setting up an evidence raid at a motel tonight. That's why I have to get back to the office. The wife's lawyers and the photog will be there to set the last-minute details."

Liddell grinned. "We better make it tomorrow night. One date with a guy in a motel should be enough for one night."

Gabby wrinkled her nose, stuck out her tongue. "You might say that's only an undress rehearsal." She pulled a mirror from the depths of her bag, inspected her appearance with apparent approval. "I'll be back at my place after midnight. Drop by for a drink, will you?"

Liddell nodded. "If I can."

72

"I'd better get on back." She got up and brushed her lips across his mouth. "Take care of yourself, baby."

The city room of the New Orleans *Dispatch* was almost deserted at 12:30. He picked his way through the organized confusion of the desks, got a passing glance from the handful of shirt-sleeved men who sat pecking away at typewriters of various ages and vintages.

He headed for a frosted glass door that was labeled "Managing Editor." Inside a man stood at the window, staring down into the street below. He turned as Liddell closed the door after him.

The man at the window was short, thick at the waist, narrow in the shoulder. His hair had once been red but had now receded until it was little more than rusty tufts over each ear. He studied Liddell from shrewd, humorous little eyes. He grinned broadly, dimples cutting white trenches into the tan of his face.

"Well, fry my hide." There was a soft Southern slur to his *i*'s. "I thought sure Gabby was pulling my leg." He stuck out his hand and returned Liddell's handshake with a firm grip. "How long you been back in our fair city, Johnny?"

"Don't you read your own sheet?"

Dunlop made a humorous face. "There's a limit to what a man will do for a buck, Johnny. Matter of fact, I've been out of town the past couple of days. Flew over to Baton Rouge on a legislative story, just got back." He walked behind his desk, flipped open the copy of the *Dispatch* on his desk, stopped at the story about the hotel shooting. His eyes jumped from line to line. He chuckled deep in his chest, then looked up. "Looks like business is going to pick up. Liddell in town hardly a day and the shootin' starts." He sat down behind the desk and motioned for Liddell to pull up a chair. "Gabby didn't make no sense on the phone, but she sounded awful interestin'. What's goin' on?"

Liddell pulled a chair up to the desk and watched with interest while the newspaperman pulled a half-empty fifth of bourbon from his bottom drawer and set it on the desk. "You got the flash that Brother Alfred's been killed?"

Dunlop transferred his gaze from the bottle to Liddell, nodded. "In a wreck of some kind. I picked it up on the teletype as I came in. Too bad. Alive he was juicy copy; missing he was even juicier. Dead?" He shrugged. "You're younger than me, Johnny. Get a couple of those paper cups by the cooler, will you?"

Liddell grunted his way to his feet and crossed the room to where a water cooler stood humming to itself. He pulled three cups from the dispenser, filled one with water, set them down on the desk. "Suppose he was murdered?"

"Very good copy indeed." He unscrewed the cap from the bourbon, poured a stiff peg into each of the empty glasses, added a touch of water from the third. "You interest me."

"I intended to. Suppose the sheriff and some of his more influential friends were determined that it be written off as an accident?"

"And you could prove different?"

"I could prove different."

The white trenches dug deep crescents into Larry Dunlop's cheeks. "Then we'd have to contradict the sheriff and his influential friends, wouldn't we?" He picked up one of the paper cups, held it up. "Here's to contradiction!"

74

Liddell picked up his cup, tasted the bourbon, and set the cup back on the desk. "Who've you got on the story?"

"As of now? Me." Dunlop drained his cup. "That is, of course, if you can prove to me that it was murder and not accident." He spilled some more bourbon into his cup. "You know this Brother Alfred for all his glory shouting wasn't exactly a sedentary character. Although I've never heard of him doing any boozing."

"How about dope?"

Dunlop shrugged. "Wouldn't surprise me none. He was a weird-looking character—"

"I know. I've seen him."

Dunlop stared at the private detective. "I thought you just got into town, that you were hired to find him?"

Liddell nodded. "I had a call in the middle of the night. From this Wanda babe who stands in for Alfred. She set up a date for me to meet him."

"Where?"

"In the middle of City Park."

Dunlop's eyes reflected his interest. "Did he show?"

"He showed, all right. We were all set to have a nice *Kaffeeklatsch* when the house fell in. I was sapped." Liddell rubbed the back of his head ruefully. "By the time I snapped out of it, there was no sign of him."

"What time was this?"

"About four or four thirty."

Dunlop considered it, grunted. "He showed no signs of being snooted?"

Liddell shook his head. "From the looks of his eyes, he might have had a skinful of C."

Dunlop leaned back in his chair and laced pudgy fingers behind his head. "Go on."

75

Liddell dug into his pocket and pulled out the remains of the horn-rimmed spectacles, dropped them on Dunlop's desk. "I found these scuffed into the mud near where I was sapped. Looks like he put up one helluva fight."

The newspaperman picked up a piece of the lens, rotated it back and forth. "I begin to get the idea. He couldn't have been doing much driving without these." He scowled at the shattered lens, scratched at his bald pate. "Who do you figure's behind this, Johnny?"

"Marty Kirk. He brought me down from New York to find this Brother Alfred. Swore that he wasn't using me to bird-dog. I figure he had me followed when I went out to keep the date with Alfred, sapped me, and set Alfred up for the phony accident."

Dunlop sipped at his paper cup, considered it. "It's an awful sucker play if it backfires. Kirk had more to gain by Alfred being knocked off than anybody else at first glance."

"He didn't expect it to backfire."

"It hasn't yet, you know." The newspaperman drained his cup, crumpled it, tossed it at the wastebasket. "That business about the glasses is interesting. But it's not conclusive. Maybe Alfred saw you getting sapped, got scared, ran for his car. Glasses or no glasses he knew he had to get away, so he took off. Because he had no glasses, he didn't see a turn, piled into a tree."

"Makes a good story," Liddell conceded.

Dunlop shrugged. "Just as good a story as accusing somebody of murdering him. And not half as libelous." He rubbed the heel of his hand along his chin and shook his head reluctantly. "You make a good case for a reasonable doubt, but it'll take more than that. A lot more."

"Look, Larry. You're already in town. Take a ride out

76

to the morgue with me. I still have one card up my sleeve. If that doesn't work," he shrugged, "then I'm licked. If it does, you've got a story."

Dunlop nodded. "O.K., I'm in for the ride over. You prove to me that Alfred was murdered, and I'm in all the way. Fair enough?"

Liddell drank on it.

8.

THE MORGUE at San Vincente was in the basement of the parish hospital. A long corridor ran from the emergency entrance ramp to a double door stenciled "Medical Examiner."

Liddell and Dunlop pushed through the doors and entered a brightly lighted office painted a sterile white. A thin man wearing a starched white jacket sat behind a metal desk making entries in a ledger. The bright light reflected off his shiny pate and face.

He looked up as the two men came in, and seemed glad of an excuse to put the pen down. He fished a rumpled handkerchief from his hip pocket and polished his bald head with a circular swabbing motion.

"Looking for someone?" His voice sounded rusty, as if it didn't get much use.

"Accident case this morning. Guy burned up in a car." Dunlop flipped a press card in front of the attendant. "Got him in here?"

The attendant swabbed his face with the handkerchief, nodded.

"Got a make on him?" Dunlop asked.

The man behind the desk pulled open a small file

78

index, nodded. "His name's Brother Alfred. Ran some kind of a temple around here someplace."

"Who identified the body?" Liddell wanted to know.

The attendant looked from Dunlop to Liddell and back again questioningly. Dunlop nodded. "He's with me."

The attendant shrugged, referred to the index card. "Some dame. Gave her name as Wanda. No surname. Seems those people only have front names." He dropped the card back, shut the file. "Want to see him?"

Liddell nodded.

"Ain't much of him left to see." The attendant grunted. He pulled himself to his feet and limped around the desk. "Come with me."

He led the way to a heavy door set in the far wall and tugged it open. Beyond was a high-ceilinged, stone-floored, unheated room with double tiers of metal lockers. Each locker had its own stenciled number.

Liddell wrinkled his nose as the blast of hot, carbolic-laden air enveloped them. There was no word spoken as they followed the thin man across the floor to the rear of the windowless room.

He yanked on one of the metal drawers; it pulled out with a screech. A piece of canvas that bulged suggestively covered its contents. The attendant reached up and pulled on a high-powered light in an enamel reflector. He grabbed a corner of the canvas, pulled it back, exposing the blackened charred remains of what had once been a man.

Its legs were blackened stumps, most of the face had been burned away. No one had bothered to close the eyes if there were any lids left, and the whites showed as he stared up into the night. The hands were twisted claws at the end of badly seared arms.

79

"Not very pretty, is he?" the attendant commented. The phone in the inside office started pealing. The attendant swore under his breath. "Damn thing always rings when you're nowhere near it." He nodded at the body. "Got enough?"

"You go ahead and answer your phone. We'll wait."

The attendant seemed undecided, shrugged. "Guess you can't walk off with him." He grinned, showing the stumps of yellowed teeth. "Be right back."

His bad leg clip-clopped across the floor as he hurried to answer the phone.

Dunlop shook his head sadly. "If it was a kill, they sure did a good job of it, Johnny. There's not enough left of him to prove a thing."

"Maybe. Maybe not." Johnny Liddell pulled a small vial of powder from his pocket. "On the way to your office, I stopped by the hotel to pick this up. Rhodokrit. Know how it works?"

Dunlop took the vial, examined it, handed it back. "Never even heard of it."

"We use it quite a lot in arson investigation," Liddell explained. "You dump it on a surface that's suspected of having been doused down with kerosene or gasoline or any other fat-dissolving inflammable compound. It turns red if they're present."

Dunlop nodded. "In other words, if this character was torched, when you put that powder on him, it should turn red?"

Liddell nodded. He unscrewed the cap of the vial, poured some of the powder into his hand. Then he leaned over the thing on the table and spilled some onto its face. The powder turned red. He repeated the process on the hands and legs, got a positive reaction.

Dunlop took a deep breath through his mouth, let it

out slowly from his nostrils. "Well, what do you know?" He took the vial of rhodokrit from Liddell, poured some into his own hand, dusted it on the body. The powder turned red wherever it fell.

"Well?" Liddell wanted to know.

"You just got yourself a boy." They waited until the attendant had limped across the floor. They slipped him a folded bill. "Thanks, pal. Where's there a phone?"

The attendant pulled the canvas sheet over the body and slammed the door back into place with a clang that reverberated throughout the entire room. "Out in the corridor. The far end." He smoothed out the bill, folded it into quarters, stuck it into his watch pocket. "Anything else I can do for you gents? We got us a pretty one in last night. Young, too. Took a hot shot or overdose, looks like. Want to see her? Real pretty," he leered.

Liddell shook his head. "Not today. We've had our quota." He fell into step beside Dunlop, and they walked back to the corridor. "Narcotics big here?"

"Getting bigger all the time," the newspaperman grunted. "Why?"

Liddell shrugged. "A young kid on a slab from an overdose. A tea party I sat in on last night. This Alfred character with a skinful when I met him. It adds up to a hot town for the shovers."

Dunlop nodded, led the way to the telephone booths. He dropped a coin, dialed the number of the *Dispatch*.

"This is Dunlop. Get me Eddie Connolly." He held his hand over the mouthpiece. "All hell is going to pop when this story breaks." He grinned. He turned his attention back to the mouthpiece. "Connolly? I've got a pip. Brother Alfred was murdered."

The receiver started to sputter metallically.

81

"I know all about that. I'm out at the morgue now. He was murdered. Now, don't tip our hand on this one, but start digging. How do I know it was murder?" He winked at Liddell. "We gave the body the rhodokrit test."

The receiver chattered back at him.

"What the hell kind of a reporter are you? What do you mean what is rhodokrit?" he barked into the receiver. "Rhodokrit is always used in suspected arson. Brother Alfred was doused down with kerosene or gasoline, set afire, and his car wrecked."

The man on the other end sounded jubilant.

"Of course it's a good story. It's a pip. Now you get started on it and see what you can do with it." He tossed the receiver back on its hook, stepped out of the phone booth. "By this time tomorrow, there won't be a soul in Louisiana who doesn't know Brother Alfred was murdered!" He caught Liddell by the arm, headed for the exit to the street.

Two big men in civilian clothes lounged outside the emergency entrance to the hospital. They looked up as Liddell and the newspaperman emerged. They couldn't have been more recognizable if they'd worn sandwich boards labeling them "Cop." The taller of the two, a big man in a rumpled blue suit and a gray fedora, stopped picking his teeth long enough to ask, "You the guys just been down to see the D.O.A.?"

Liddell nodded. "Yeah. Why?"

The man in the blue suit went back to picking his teeth. "Sheriff wants to see you." He nodded his head at the building across the way.

"Some other time," Dunlop told him. "I've got a paper to get out." He started to shoulder past. A hamlike hand caught his arm and spun him around.

"The sheriff says he wants to see you now." The big man screwed his face into what passed for a smile. "He's not particular what condition you come in."

Liddell started to interfere, but the newspaperman shook his head. "Let's go over and see the sheriff, Johnny. If you're going to work around here, you'll have to meet him sooner or later." He picked the plain-clothes man's hand off his arm. "I know the way."

"We'll trail along just to make sure you don't get lost." The man in the blue suit nodded.

They crossed the street and entered a low white stone building. The sheriff's office was at the end of the first corridor. The two plain-clothes men followed them to the door and took up a position in the hall.

Sheriff Lalonde sat behind an oversized, varnished desk, eying the two men with no signs of enthusiasm. He reached out for a pack of cigarettes on the end of his desk and dumped one out.

"Hear you were over taking a look at the body?" He directed his attention to Dunlop. "What's on your mind?"

"News. That's my business. Alfred's death is news."

The sheriff moved his eyes over to Liddell. "What's your business?"

"I'm a private detective." Liddell dumped his credentials on the sheriff's desk.

Lalonde dropped his eyes to the papers, riffled through them, snorted. "What were you doing over there?"

"Just looking." Liddell picked up his papers, rearranged them, and shoved them back into his breast pocket. "I was hired to find Brother Alfred. I was just looking out for a client's interests."

"You were hired to find him." He scratched a paper match along the abrasive strip on the box, held it to his cigarette. "You found him. How soon will you be leaving?"

Liddell shrugged. "As soon as I know who killed Alfred."

Sheriff Lalonde's eyes flicked from one man to the other. "He killed himself. He got a skinful of liquor, drove his car into a tree." His voice dropped dangerously. "Maybe I didn't make myself very clear, Liddell. We don't like peepers around here. We don't like anybody that stirs up trouble." His eyes rolled back to the newspaperman. "This Brother Alfred pulled a fake disappearance for reasons of his own, went on a binge. He got a snootful and hit a tree. That's the way it stands on the record."

Dunlop stuck his chin out. "That's your story."

"That's the official story." The sheriff put his hands flat on the desk and lifted himself out of his chair. "That's the story the papers will print. Yours included."

"Not the *Dispatch*. The *Dispatch* will print that he was murdered."

The sheriff's face turned a deep red, then darkened to purple. A little vein in the center of his forehead started to throb, and the corners of his mouth twitched. "You might have to prove that crack, Dunlop."

"I might be able to," Dunlop snapped back.

Lalonde stamped around the desk and planted himself in front of the two men. He waved a stubby forefinger under their noses. "Get this straight, Dunlop. Alfred was killed in an accident." The sheriff bared his teeth in an ugly, crooked grin. "Accidents can happen to anybody. You understand? He was killed in an accident!"

"Wouldn't you like to hear why the *Dispatch* is going to charge that he was murdered?" Dunlop asked quietly.

84

Lalonde pounded his desk with a clenched fist. "Stop saying that! I don't want theories or guesses. You couldn't prove he was murdered! Neither can anyone else. There's not enough left of him to prove anything except that he's dead!"

"You don't need much to prove an accident was faked," Liddell put in. "There's enough left to prove that."

The sheriff whirled on him. "You stay out of this, peeper! You have no standing in this parish. Start getting in my hair and I have a couple of boys who are dying to find out how tough these New York eyes really are."

"Maybe they better start trying. Because I'm the guy who convinced Dunlop that Alfred was murdered. And if your coroner brings in any other verdict, Dunlop's paper has enough evidence of murder to make the verdict look silly."

The sheriff's red-rimmed eyes played hopscotch from Liddell to the newspaperman and back. "Convince me." He wet his lips with a quick dart of his tongue, tried to swallow his fury, failed miserably. "I got an open mind. Convince me."

Liddell dug into his pocket, pulled out the little vial of powder. "There's all the proof you need."

Lalonde stared at the vial. "What the hell are you trying to pull?" he roared. "What can that prove?"

"That Brother Alfred was torched, and that he was probably dead before he ever got into that car." He tossed the vial up, caught it. "Sprinkle a little of this on any surface that's been doused with an inflammable oil for torching, and it turns red. We tried a little on the body. Wherever it touched, it turned red. He was soaked with either kerosene or gasoline before the fire."

85

Beads of perspiration glistened on the sheriff's fore-head and upper lip. He started to say something, changed his mind, wiped the wet smear of his mouth with the back of his hand. He jabbed at a button on the desk. The door opened, and the plain-clothes man in the rumpled blue suit stood in the doorway.

"Need me, sheriff?" He grinned, licked his lips, and looked Liddell over.

The sheriff nodded. He didn't take his eyes off Dunlop. "Get over and find the coroner. Tell him maybe he better hold up his verdict on that Brother Alfred accident. The *Dispatch* thinks he was murdered."

9.

THE ROAD between the parish offices at San Vincente and New Orleans was recovered land, built over the marshland that dipped below the road level on either side.

Larry Dunlop kept the little sedan in the middle of the road, pushed the needle to between fifty and sixty, and kept it there.

"Nice character, your Sheriff Lalonde." Liddell grunted. "Never lets facts interfere with his preconceived conclusion, does he?"

Dunlop grinned. "We've got our share of that kind in the outlying parishes. By and large, though, we're managing to straighten them out. Lalonde is particularly well set with a machine like Marty Kirk's in back of him."

Liddell watched the majestic, low-branched oaks sweeping past his window. "City authorities have no power over here, eh?"

"No. The parish sheriff is top man." Dunlop kept looking into his rear-view mirror, pushed the accelerator down farther. The light car swayed ominously.

Liddell braced himself against the door on his side.

"Where's the fire, Larry? These roads and this car weren't built for speed."

"A car back there." He flicked his eyes at the rearview mirror. "It's been creeping up on us."

Liddell swung around in his seat and looked out the back window. A big black sedan was slowly closing down the distance between them. There appeared to be two men in the front seat, none in the back.

"Maybe they're in a hurry. Slow down and see," Liddell suggested.

Dunlop eased the pressure on the accelerator, and the little car slowed down. The car behind showed no signs of cutting its speed.

"They're not following us or they would have slowed down, too," Liddell told him. "Pull over and give them room."

Dunlop edged slowly toward the side of the road; the big car roared up and came abreast. It edged up until its front fender was even with that of the small car. Then, the driver of the big car swung his wheel. There was a grinding of metal as the fenders met, the screeching of tires as Dunlop tried to apply his brakes.

The little car swung toward the embankment. Dunlop fought to gain control as it slewed from side to side. Suddenly its front outside wheel slipped off the pavement, sank into a soft shoulder. The car teetered sickeningly, went over. It plunged down the hill, end over end, and came to rest with a shattering crash against the trunk of a huge oak.

The black sedan roared on toward New Orleans.

' It seemed as if endless time had passed before consciousness came knocking at Johnny Liddell's skull. From somewhere close he heard the rumble of voices; the

88

acrid smell of gasoline stung his nostrils. He tried to move, found himself pinned down by some heavy weight. He called out weakly.

One of the voices seemed to come closer. "Hey, one of them's alive. We better get them out."

There was a flurry of activity, and then the weight that pinned him against the bottom of the car was removed. None too gentle hands reached in, grabbed Liddell under the arms, lifted him out of the car.

The car itself lay on its side, its roof smashed in by the trunk of the tree. Larry Dunlop's body lay alongside the car, a pulpy red mass where the head had been.

Liddell wiped his mouth with the back of his hand and leaned against the car. The highway patrolman who had dragged him from the wreck stood by, watching him. One of them dug into his tunic pocket and came up with a cigarette.

"A smoke help, Mac?" he asked.

Liddell nodded gratefully as the highway patrolman stuck a cigarette between his lips and lit it. He waited until he had the cigarette going, until he had sucked in a lungful of smoke and let it out slowly. "Get the guys who did it?"

The two patrolmen exchanged glances. "What guys?" The shorter of the two looked down at Dunlop. "There's the guy that did it. Skid marks on the road show he was weaving all over the place."

"We were pushed off the road." He looked from one patrolman to the other, recognized the disbelief in their face, and shrugged. "O.K., have it your way." He staggered around the smashed car and sat down with his back to the big tree.

A searing flash of pain shot through his head, and he

identified it as the screech of a siren. After a moment, a car with two red headlights skidded to a stop on the road above.

One of the highway patrolmen scrambled up the hill, saluted the man in the car, reported in a low voice. The car door opened, and Sheriff Lalonde stepped out. He came down the hill, bent over the body of Larry Dunlop, snorted. Then he stiff-legged it to where Liddell sat propped against the tree.

"Well, well. I didn't figure I'd have the pleasure of meeting you again so soon." He reached over, grabbed Liddell by the lapels, pulled him to his feet, and shoved him back against the tree. "Drunken driving, eh?"

"The other fellow was behind the wheel, sheriff—" the shorter of the highway patrolmen started to say.

The sheriff whirled on him, his washed-out eyes gleaming red in the reflected light of the headlights. "When I want to hear from you, I'll ask." He nodded his dismissal. "My boys will take care of it from here on. You'll make your report directly to me."

The patrolman touched two fingers to the shiny visor of his cap. He waved for his companion and started up the incline toward his car. Lalonde waited until the patrol car had zoomed off, then walked over to where the newspaperman lay and turned the body over with his toe contemptuously. "The power of the press!" he snorted. "You see, Carroll?" He grinned at a beefy man who stood with him. "Newspaper guys bleed just like us poor humans!"

Johnny Liddell finished his cigarette, dropped it to the ground, and crushed it with his heel. "We were pushed off the road, sheriff. Two guys in a black sedan."

Lalonde grinned at him. He walked back, stood in front of Liddell, and rocked on the balls of his feet.

"That's not the way we heard it. Dunlop there was on his way back to town, and he hit a soft shoulder." The sheriff shrugged. "Bad road, happens all the time. The parish ought to do something about it."

"Too bad it didn't happen that way, sheriff," Liddell grunted. "I guess you were forgetting I was with him."

Lalonde grinned at him. "No. But you're going to."

Sheriff Lalonde sat behind the desk in his office, an unlit cigar between his teeth. He studied Johnny Liddell across the desk.

"I told you before I don't like troublemakers. Dunlop was alone in the car when he hit that soft shoulder." He rolled the unlit cigar in the center of his mouth between thumb and forefinger. "And you're finished with what you came to do, so you'll be on your way tomorrow. I'll have a couple of boys tuck you in tonight and escort you to the airport. We wouldn't want you to think we wasn't hospitable."

Liddell grinned frostily. "I wouldn't want you to go to all that trouble, sheriff. Especially since I'm not going anywhere."

Lalonde rocked in his desk chair, sank his teeth into the end of the cigar. "That's what you think. You're either going back where you came from, or you're going to sit it out in one of those cells until you get smart."

"On what charge?"

"Drunken driving. I just remember how it happened. You and Dunlop were carousing around all afternoon. On the way back, you started to hit it up, lost control, caused Dunlop's death." He pulled the cigar from between his teeth, jabbed it at Liddell. "And as justice of the peace, I can toss you in the poky for so long you won't even remember your right name."

91

"You couldn't make it stick."

Lalonde grinned at him. "When a man pleads guilty, it's my duty to save the parish the cost of a trial." He slammed the desk with the flat of his hand. "That's the way it goes if you get tough." He jabbed the button on the desk, the door opened. The thick-necked plain-clothes man in the rumpled blue suit walked in.

"Yeah, chief." He rubbed the knuckles of his right hand into his left palm and licked his lips. "Do we take him?"

The sheriff shrugged. "Depends on him, Carroll. If he gets smart, decides to go back where he came from, we give him a lift back to town."

Liddell pulled a crumpled pack of cigarettes from his pocket, held it up. "O.K. to smoke?"

"Sure. This isn't a third degree. We're all sitting around trying to get at the truth."

Liddell grunted, stuck a cigarette between his lips, lit it. The big man in the blue suit stepped over, smacked it out of his mouth before he could fill his lungs.

"Don't overdo it, pal. Smoking's bad for the wind. And you're likely to need all you got." He towered over Liddell, grinning down at him expectantly.

"Well, peeper? Decided?" Sheriff Lalonde sounded bored. "What does it read on the disposition? Accident while driving alone, or death as the result of a drunken driving accident?"

"Neither. Make it murder."

The big man in the blue suit swung his beefy hand in an arc, caught Liddell across the face, knocked him out of his chair. "You just said a dirty word," he chided. He looked over at the sheriff. "I got a feeling he's going to plead guilty, chief."

Lalonde nodded. "You don't have to worry about

marking him up. As long as he was in an accident, he might as well look like it."

Carroll walked to the door, opened it, stuck his head out. After a moment another big man came to the door. Carroll whispered to him, they both walked over, grabbed Liddell by the arms, and dragged him out of the office.

The squad room was down a flight from the sheriff's office. It had no windows, its walls were plain cinder block painted a dun-colored brown. The door was thick, fitted so closely it made the room practically sound-proof.

Carroll pushed the door open, waited until his partner had dragged Liddell in, then closed the door. He loosened his tie and shucked off his jacket. His partner pushed Liddell into a wooden chair, pulled a blackjack from his hip pocket, slammed it against the heel of his hand suggestively.

Liddell sagged in the chair, pretended to be semi-conscious. The man with the blackjack grabbed him by the hair, pulled his head back, sneered.

"He's almost passed out with fright, Carroll. I thought these private eyes were hard boys. Hell, you bring in a nigger from the canefield, he gives you more exercise'n this one will." He dropped Liddell's head disgustedly.

Carroll flat-footed over to where Liddell sat, caught him by the necktie, pulled him to his feet. Liddell's head rolled uncontrollably. The plain-clothes man slashed at the side of Liddell's face, knocked him to his knees. He kicked out at his face, Liddell rolled with the kick, took it in the shoulder, fell back to the floor.

Carroll spat down at him, stood over him, hands on hip, feet astraddle. "No fight at all. Well, the chief says mark him up." He raised his foot to kick at Liddell's face, was momentarily off-balance.

Liddell put everything into a sudden upward thrust of his heels, felt them sink into the big man's groin. Carroll's eyes popped, and his face went an ugly purple. He sank to his knees, gasped noisily for breath, tumbled forward, hit the stone floor face first with an ugly plop.

The second plain-clothes man was stunned by the suddenness of the move. Before he could gather his wits, Liddell was on his feet. The cop tried to swing the sap up, but Liddell hit him a paralyzing chop above the wrist. The blackjack fell to the floor.

Liddell straightened up, wiped the perspiration from his upper lip with the back of his hand. Then he started to move in. He missed a hard left, took a staggering right to the side of his head that started bells ringing, bright lights flashing. He shook his head, cleared it in time to see the sheriff's man going for his hip holster. Before the gun could clear leather, Liddell was all over him. He caught the gun hand in a viselike grip, held it bent in back of the other man.

The deputy struggled, tried to bring his knee up, lost leverage as Liddell stuck the top of his head under the deputy's chin, pushing it upward and backward. Perspiration broke out in gleaming beads all over the deputy's face as slowly, inexorably Liddell bent him back over his own arm. The sheriff's man screamed out in pain; the gun slipped from his damp fingers and hit the floor. Liddell sent it spinning to the corner of the room with a kick.

Liddell released his hammer lock on the plain-clothes man, let him fall to the ground. He sat there, rubbing his wrist, glaring at the private detective. Then he reached up, slipped his upper plate out of his mouth, dropped it into his jacket pocket. He dragged himself to his feet, crouched, waited. He stood between Liddell and the gun at the other end of the room.

Liddell started to circle around him toward the gun. The deputy moved with surprising speed for a man his size. He darted forward, sank his left into Liddell's stomach, took a smashing right to the eye in return. He took the punch well, kept boring in. Liddell back-pedaled, made the bigger man come to him. Suddenly, without warning, he stopped his backward movement, planted his feet, lashed out with both hands.

The maneuver caught the plain-clothes man off balance. He took a straight overhand to the jaw, an upper-cut to the throat that made him gag. Liddell continued to throw both hands, sank his left to the cuff in the other man's middle. The deputy retched, gasped wide-mouthed for air.

Liddell moved in. He crossed his right to the other man's unprotected jaw. The deputy's eyes turned glassy; he made a feeble effort to lash out at Liddell but seemed to have lost all co-ordination. Liddell chopped at the side of the big man's neck, the man's knees folded under him, and he hit the floor with a thud. He lay there, face down, and didn't move.

Liddell walked over to the sink in the corner, stuck his face under the cold tap, washed the fuzziness from his brain. He picked up the gun from against the wall, walked over to where Carroll lay, still out cold. He turned him over, tugged his .38 from its shoulder holster.

He was straightening up when the door to the squad room burst open. Liddell crouched, with the two guns leveled at the doorway.

Sheriff Lalonde stood in the doorway, his eyes popping. He looked from Liddell to his two fallen deputies and back. His lips moved, but no sound came out.

"Come on in and join the party, sheriff," Liddell panted at him.

The sheriff eyed the two guns in Liddell's hands, stepped in with alacrity. Standing behind him was a thin man with a gray fedora perched on the back of his head. He was lean, gray-haired. He had sharp, inquisitive features.

"I'm Ed Connolly, Larry Dunlop's assistant." He answered the unspoken question in Liddell's eyes. "I got here as soon as I could."

"What brought you out?"

Connolly grinned. "I got a call from a gal named Gabby Benton. She told me you were with Larry when the accident happened. The sheriff's man said Larry was alone. I thought I better have a look."

"You misunderstood my deputy," the sheriff growled.

Connolly ignored the sheriff and looked around curiously. "What's been going on down here?"

"The sheriff and his boys were betting I'd keep my mouth shut about being in the car with Dunlop. They lost."

Lalonde waved it aside impatiently. "I knew nothing about it." He glared down at Carroll, who was beginning to moan his way back to consciousness. "When they brought Liddell in, he was drunk and violent. They took him down here to quiet him down."

"He must've gotten real quiet, sheriff," Connolly growled. "Looks like your boys went to sleep on the job."

The sheriff grunted, walked over to the sink, filled a metal bucket with cold water, walked back, spilled it over the unconscious deputies.

Carroll groaned, tried to make his feet, doubled up,

and stretched out on his face. The other man barely stirred. The sheriff turned to Liddell, snapped at him. "You're free to go now. If we want any testimony, we'll get in touch with you."

Liddell looked from the sheriff to Connolly quizzically. "What gives?"

"The sheriff tells me the accident was caused by a reckless driver who cut Larry off. The car got out of control, went off the road. Check?"

"That was no reckless driver. That guy deliberately forced us off the road."

The sheriff snorted impatiently. "You can't go around making these unfounded accusations around here. Can you describe the driver or give us a license number?"

Liddell shook his head. "It happened too fast."

Lalonde nodded. "So fast you couldn't be sure whether it was deliberate or not. If we find the driver, you can have a look at him. But I think it'll be mighty hard to find a guy you can't even describe." He turned to the newspaperman. "Why should anyone want to kill Dunlop? We all liked him."

"One reason might be because he was going to spill the story that Alfred was murdered and torched."

The sheriff rolled his eyes at the ceiling. "Listen to that one." He shook his head at Liddell. "Maybe I ought to have Doc Lane take a look at you, Liddell. You've got murder on the brain. First poor Larry. Now Brother Alfred."

"Dunlop called in a story. Said he had proof that Alfred was murdered," Connolly put in.

"First I ever heard of it," the sheriff shrugged. "If you can show me how you can tell he was murdered, I'll have the coroner reopen the case."

"I can show you, and you know it," Liddell snarled.

97

"I'll be glad to see it. And in front of our newspaper friend. So if you're right, he'll have a good story. Won't he?"

Liddell scowled at the note of confidence in the sheriff's voice. "Suppose we go over to the morgue and try?"

The sheriff held his hands out, palms up. "I'll be glad to have you drop into my morgue any time."

"You can say that again," Liddell grunted.

Conversation was suspended as the three men crossed the road from the sheriff's office to the parish morgue. The same thin man was sitting behind the same white desk making entries into the same ledger. He looked up as the sheriff stalked in, pasted an obsequious smile on his face.

"Some people here want to have a look at that auto accident case. The fellow they call Brother Alfred."

The thin man bobbed his head. "Sure, sheriff."

"Anything been done to that body since I was here?" Liddell wanted to know.

The bald-headed man behind the desk turned blank eyes on him. "When were you here, mister? I don't remember ever seeing you."

Liddell growled deep in his throat. "I was here with Larry Dunlop of the *Dispatch*. You showed us Alfred's body." He broke off, stared at the man. "You're sure I was never here?"

The attendant mopped at his bald head with a dingy handkerchief, looked to the sheriff. "I don't know what this is all about, sheriff. I never even saw this man before."

Liddell leaned the flat of his hands on the corner of the desk, stuck his face within inches of the attendant's. "Then how come I can lead you right to the drawer he's in?"

The man in the white suit's Adam's apple bobbed fitfully. "I don't know, mister. Maybe you're psychic or something." He looked to the sheriff again. "I never showed him."

"Well, let's go in and let Liddell take us to the body," the sheriff nodded. He turned on his heel, led the way to the big door, waited until the attendant pushed it open, held it. "Which way, Liddell?"

"All the way in the back. The next to last tier, second drawer up."

"That right?" The sheriff snapped at the attendant.

The man in the white jacket shook his head. "He's here in this first tier off the door. The bottom drawer." He clip-clopped across the floor, pulled open the bottom drawer, pulled back the canvas. The charred body he had seen earlier stared up at Liddell.

"Well?" Lalonde made no attempt to hide his pleasure.

"Maybe I've been underestimating you, sheriff," Liddell nodded. "I suppose you've also foreseen this." Liddell dug into his pocket, brought out the vial of rhodokrit.

"What's that?" the sheriff asked with polite interest.

Liddell turned to Connolly. "Dunlop told you about the test we made with rhodokrit?"

The newsman nodded. "I don't know how it works, though."

"You sprinkle it on a surface that's been doused with an inflammable oil and it turns red." He spilled some on his hand, powdered it over the body. There was no reaction.

"Check and checkmate," Liddell nodded.

"It didn't work?" The sheriff asked solicitously.

Liddell capped the vial, dropped it into his pocket.

"The body's probably been washed down with alcohol or some other compound that breaks down the reaction."

"We've got to kill the story?" Connolly asked.

Liddell nodded. "For the time being." He turned, stared at Lalonde impersonally. "This is your round, sheriff. But I'll be back."

"Do that," the sheriff nodded. "Come back to our morgue any time. Sometime when you can stay."

10.

GABBY BENTON stretched out on the divan on her sundeck, watching Johnny Liddell making the drinks. He handed one to her, sat on the edge of the divan with her, and stared out over the small park beyond and the low roofs of the older section of the city.

"You look mighty romantic with that piece of adhesive over your eye, Johnny. Really swashbuckling," she grinned.

"I guess if it hadn't been for your calling Connolly to get out there and make like the Marines, I'd be covered with adhesive."

Gabby snorted. "Not from what I heard. If I'd known they only sicked two men on you, I wouldn't even have bothered. I thought you were really outnumbered."

Liddell grinned, took a swallow from his glass.

"What are you thinking, Johnny?" the blonde wanted to know.

"About the city out there."

Gabby got up on her elbow, looked out over the railing. "Beautiful, isn't it?"

Liddell nodded. "Makes you wonder how anything so beautiful can contain so much that's evil." He got up from the divan, walked over to the ornamental grill-

101

work railing, and looked down. "You know, this is the way I've felt ever since I got into this damn town."

"What do you mean?"

"Up in the air." He shook his head, took a drink from his glass. "It makes less and less sense all the time."

"You don't have to worry about it any more. You did what you came for. You found Alfred—"

"And set him up for the kill."

Gabby shook her head. "But you've got no case. You've got to have a victim before you can have a murder. As it stands right now, Alfred died in an accident."

"That doesn't alter the fact that Marty Kirk murdered him."

Gabby sighed. "I think you're wrong, Johnny. Honestly, I know what goes on behind the scenes in this town a little better than you do. I believe Kirk when he says he had no reason to want Alfred dead. Alfred is no good to him dead."

"Why?"

"Let me do a little guessing, a combination of rumors and facts." She cupped her glass in her hands, stared down into it. "Marty represents the syndicate down here. Part of his job is to push a set quota of narcotics. Alfred runs the temple, one of the biggest dope drops along the Gulf. All of a sudden, Alfred takes off, disappears without warning. Maybe he disappears owing Marty a lot of money, hasn't paid for his supplies."

"Aren't you building a case for a hit?"

Gabby looked up, shook her head. "If Alfred is killed, Marty never gets his money. If he stays alive, there's always a chance."

Liddell kicked it around, found no soft spot. "O.K.,

just for the sake of argument, Kirk didn't kill Alfred. Who did?"

Gabby shook her head. "According to the coroner, nobody."

"I tell you we had proof he was torched. I can't prove it with Dunlop dead, but I know what I saw. Alfred was murdered whether the proof will stand up or not."

Gabby patted the divan by her side. "Why get yourself all stewed up? There's nothing you can do about it when the cards are stacked the way they are over the line there."

Liddell took a deep breath, blew it out through pursed lips. "They certainly play rings around me in this league, Gabby. It's beginning to get under my skin." He dropped down alongside her, shook his head dolefully.

Gabby laid her hand on his knee. "You're crazy to let it. You were hired to find a man. So he turns up dead—"

"And another guy who did nothing to anybody turns up the same way because he wanted to help me."

"Another accident."

"Another accident." Liddell got up, stamped to the rail, swung around. "I'm crazy to let it get under my skin, you say? Do you know what's happened to me since I got off that damn plane? I've been bawled out by a D.A., threatened by a sheriff, fired by a gangster, beaten up by goons. Not to mention the guy who climbed my balcony, and it wasn't to wherefore art thou, Romeo, either. And what have I got to show for it? Bumps on my head!"

Gabby struggled to keep a straight face and lost. "I don't mean to laugh, Johnny. But it sounds so funny the way you say it. None of what's happened's been your fault. The breaks were just against you."

"In the meantime, Kirk's sitting back like an overfed spider, getting a big bang out of the run-around I'm getting."

"I'm not too sure Marty's getting any bang out of this whole deal. If Alfred did skip out with some of Marty's money, it wasn't pennies. And the big boys in the syndicate are going to expect to be paid their share either way."

Liddell grunted. "Well, I would feel a little better if I could persuade myself he's doing a little sweating, too." He checked his watch. "Can I call my hotel?"

Gabby nodded. "They'll be glad to hear from you. I tried to reach you, and the clerk sounded as if he were going to cry."

Liddell grinned, drained his glass, set it down on the end table, walked in to the telephone. He dialed the number and held the instrument to his ear. The switchboard girl connected him with the front desk.

"I'm so glad you called in, Mr. Liddell. There is a lady been trying very hard to reach you. She called four times in two hours."

Liddell nodded. "I know. I'm with Miss Benton now."

"But it was not Miss Benton, Mr. Liddell. She called too." There was a slight embarrassed titter over the wire. "I made a mistake when she called. I thought it was Miss Martinez, and I told her I had her three messages. Miss Benton said she hadn't left any."

"Martinez?" Liddell pinched at his nostrils. "Did she say who she was or what it was about?"

"I have the message here. Shall I read it over the phone?"

Liddell nodded. "Yeah."

" 'Most important I see you today. Please come to my
104

apartmont, Seventy Marseilles Road,' " the clerk read into the mouthpiece. "It is signed 'Angie Martinez.' "

A light seemed to flick on in Liddell's brain. Angie Martinez! The girl at the temple.

"Oh, I understand. I'll take care of it. Incidentally do you know where that address is?"

The clerk hesitated. "It is a very bad neighborhood. We call it Little San Juan. It is mostly Puerto Rican."

Liddell nodded. "O.K., thanks. I'll see you when I get back to the hotel. In the meantime, destroy that message." He dropped the receiver back on its hook, walked back to the sun deck.

"Anything important?" Gabby drawled. She nodded at his refilled glass, patted the divan.

Liddell picked up the glass, swirled the liquor over the ice. "Nothing much. A few messages. One from you, for that matter."

Gabby slid her arm around his neck, pulled his face down on her shoulder. "I don't have to leave here until around nine. Why don't we call down, have some dinner sent up, then you can rest here until I get back?"

"I'll take a rain check on it, Gabby. I've got a couple of things I want to do, a couple of people I want to see. Then, if there's no sign of a break, I may very well decide to pack the whole thing in."

Marseilles Road was Little San Juan. A long row of uniformly dingy, soot-stained, three-story brick houses stretched the full length of the block. Short flights of unwashed stone steps ran from littered sidewalks to small, dark vestibules. Loudly hooting teen-agers of both sexes chased each other into alleys and darkened doorways, scuffling sounds replacing the hooting as they disappeared into the shadow. Men and women shuffled by on the sidewalks—the men zoot-suited, colorful peacocks; the women drab, prematurely aged, tired.

Johnny Liddell melted into the slowly moving tide of white, yellow, black, and brown that ebbed and flowed along Marseilles Road. He stopped in front of Number 70, staring up at its windows with their drawn shades. The blank windows seemed to stare back at him dumbly.

He climbed the three steps to a foul-smelling vestibule. As he stepped into the semigloom, two slim figures disentangled themselves from a close embrace in the inner hall, ran giggling toward the cellar entrance in the rear.

"Chico, he very precocious," Liddell grunted. Three rusting tin mail boxes, badly battered, hung askew on the wall of the vestibule. The push buttons in the bells had disappeared long ago. He wrinkled his nose at the pungent odor compounded of equal parts of stale cooking and unwashed bodies that seemed to spill from the hallway door. He fumbled through his pockets for a cigarette, found himself out.

He stepped back out onto the stoop, stared around. On the far side of the street, he recognized the store front of a bodega. He crossed the street, shouldered his way through the slow-moving crowd.

The store was dim, dank smelling. A dirty, faded curtain cut the living quarters off from the front of the store. There was no one behind the counter. Liddell looked around at the dusty fixtures, the fly-specked showcases. A rack of magazines stood against the far wall. They were lurid, sexy, well thumbed. They were standard in one respect—every one featured a cover portrait of an unbelievably busty, blue-eyed blonde. Liddell picked one up, flipped through it, replaced it in the rack.

The curtain pushed back, and a fat old woman shuffled in. Her face was old, wrinkled, the color of walnut. She had wispy gray hair that stuck out at right angles to her skull. Her eyes narrowed as they took in the unfamiliar white face, the thick shoulders of the man in the store. She reached up and tugged on the bunch of hairs that stuck out of her chin.

"A pack of cigarettes, Chiquita," Liddell told her.

She shuffled to the showcase, pulled a pack of Chesterfields from under the counter, pushed them at him. He dropped a quarter into her palm.

"You know a girl named Martinez? Angie Martinez?"

The old woman shook her head, bared naked gums in a slack-lipped smile. "*Yo no se. No hable ingles.*" Her eyes were black, opaque buttons.

The curtain flipped again. A small dark girl came out. Her hair was thick, jet, kinky. Her mouth was smeared a bright red, her dark cheeks heavily rouged. She was high-hipped, high-breasted, wore a tight black sweater and skirt, a bright red sash.

"You looking for girl?" The heavily painted lips split, revealing a set of dingy, widely separated teeth.

Liddell nodded. "A girl named Angie Martinez."

The little black-haired girl came up closer to him, looked up into his face. "Me, Rosa, much prettier than Martinez." She swung her head to the old crone. "*Oye, es verdad, no?*"

The old woman bared her naked gums again, rocked her head.

"I'm sure you're much prettier, Rosa. But I've got to see Angie Martinez on business. Which apartment is hers?"

Rosa tossed her head angrily. "She horse face." She stuck her front teeth over her lower lip to illustrate the

107

criticism. "Why you want her? You come with me. *Que lindo tu eres.*" She rolled her eyes lasciviously.

Liddell grinned at her. "I have to talk to Martinez. If I came up here for a girl, I'd much rather have you," he assured her.

The girl pouted at him, partially mollified. "She in front apartment. But you make mistake. Me, Rosa, I much fun, *chu-chi.*"

Liddell pulled a bill from his pocket, folded it, slipped it to her. She looked at it, slipped it down the neck of her sweater into her flimsy brassière. She winked lewdly at Liddell. "You come back," she prophesied.

Back at Number 70, Liddell ran up the short flight of steps, re-entered the dark vestibule. He walked through to a flight of stairs that ran to the upper story.

The second-floor hallway was even more malodorous than the lower hall had been. He walked softly to the door of the front apartment.

He pushed the bell, heard it ring inside the apartment. There was a soft rustle of sound from the other side of the door, then silence. He waited for a second, rang again. There was no response.

Liddell bent over, peered at the lock, and took a thin strip of celluloid from his jacket pocket. He slipped it into the crack of the door, manipulated it for a moment, and was rewarded by a soft click.

He caught the knob, turned it softly, and pushed the door open. For seconds, he stood outside the opened door. Then he slid his .45 from its holster, stepped in, and closed the door behind him with his heel.

He stood, fanning the room with the gun, straining his ears for some sound or indication of life. The apartment seemed to be empty.

The room showed signs of a hasty search—the drawers

108

were hanging open, contents strewn all over the floor. The door to the bedroom beyond was ajar. Liddell crossed the living room cautiously, nosed the door open with the muzzle of the .45.

It was a small, mean bedroom. An ugly dresser leaned drunkenly against an unpainted plaster wall. An unmade double bed dominated the room, its soiled linen dingy and yellow in the half-light. This room, too, had been searched. The drawers had been pulled out, emptied. Clothes from the closet had been dumped into an untidy pile in the center of the room.

A small lamp was lit on the dresser, throwing a yellow light over the bed. Angie Martinez lay on her back across the bed. One arm dangled to the floor; the other was thrown across her face as though to ward off a blow. Her throat had been cut from ear to ear, and a pool of blood had dripped to the floor beside the bed.

Liddell's eyes flicked around the room, noted the closed window, the half-open door to the lavatory. Whoever had been in the apartment when he rang the bell was still in it. Softly he crossed the room, pushed open the lavatory door. It was empty.

"All right, you in the closet. You get a count of three, then I make a sieve out of that door. Come out, hands first. Make sure the hands are empty."

There was no sound from the closet. Liddell could feel the butt of the .45 growing moist from his palm.

"One."

There was no sign of life from the closet. The pulse in his trigger finger started to pound.

"Two!"

Liddell could feel the faint line of perspiration that beaded his forehead and upper lip. His finger grew white on the trigger.

"No, don't!" The closet door sprang open. A small pair of hands stuck out. A blonde girl followed them. She had difficulty keeping them from trembling. "Don't shoot!" she begged piteously.

Liddell walked over and poked the gun into the closet to make certain it was empty. When he turned back, the girl had sunk her face in her hands, sobbing loudly. He took her by the arm, led the way out of the bedroom, and sat her down on a wooden chair in the living room. He let her cry it out.

"You should have shot me. You should have ended it," she sobbed through her fingers. "If I weren't such a coward—" She dissolved into another burst of weeping.

"Suppose you stop crying long enough to answer a few questions?"

The blonde dropped her hands and looked up. She couldn't have been over nineteen. Her hair was a natural ash blonde, her eyes gray. Her face was drawn, drained of all color, her make-up standing out in dark patches against the pallor. Her full lower lip quivered as she looked at Liddell.

"Use a drink?" he asked gently.

Her only response was the heaving of her shoulders. After a moment, she regained control. "I'll have a cigarette if you have one."

Liddell pulled out his cigarettes, dumped out two, lit them, passed one to the girl. "You're in a bad spot, Blondie," he told her.

The girl took a deep drag on the cigarette. Her hand shook as she took it from her mouth, breathed a fog of smoke in a jerky stream. "I didn't kill her. She was like that."

Liddell nodded. "I don't think you did. A killing like
110

that's messy." He gave her a moment to compose herself. "What are you doing here?"

The shaking started again. "I—I came to see Angie. She was my friend. I—I heard you at the door. I thought you were the—the killer, so I hid." Her hand wobbled violently as she carried the cigarette back to her mouth.

Liddell shook his head. "Lying doesn't help either of us."

"I'm not lying." A tiny vein started to throb in the side of the girl's neck.

"What were you looking for?"

The girl shook her head and dropped her eyes. She started fumbling with her fingers in her lap.

"Let's try it this way. What's your name?"

"Arrest me if you like. But I'm not saying another thing."

"I'm no cop," Liddell told her.

Her eyes shot up hopefully. "Who are you? What are you doing here?" The hope drained away, leaving the eyes empty, dead. "Then you're one of them."

"I don't know what that means, but if you mean I'm one of the temple gang, I'm not." He put his hand on her shoulder, could feel her trembling. "I may be able to help you, if you'll let me."

"What about her?" She nodded toward the bedroom door.

"It's too late to help her." He stuck the .45 in its shoulder holster, caught the girl by the arm. "Maybe if we get out of here, you'll feel more like talking?"

"Where are you taking me?"

Liddell grinned at her. "No place. You take me wherever you want to go. All I want to do is talk this out with you. Won't you believe that I want to help you?"

"I want to." The girl got up. Her knees were knocking. "I need help so badly. Can we go to my place?"

Liddell nodded. "Any place you say." He led her to the door. She had perceptible difficulty in making her knees behave. "Will you just answer two questions?"

She nodded.

"Did you tear the place apart like this?"

She shook her head. "It was this way when I came in and—and found her."

Liddell nodded. "This one you don't have to answer if you don't want to. What's your name?"

The blonde looked at him. "Donna. Donna Espirito." She threw her head back proudly. "My father owns a plantation outside of Baton Rouge."

"I'm Johnny Liddell. I operate a detective agency in New York." He stuck out his hand; she shook it gravely and managed a wan smile. "Now that we're friends, let's get out of here." He led her to the staircase, down to the lower hall without meeting anybody. They walked out into the dusk of Marseilles Road.

With the coming of night, Marseilles Road was bestirring itself into activity. A few drunks, white and black, made their appearance on the street. An occasional yellow-faced girl, dressed in yellow or bright red, started on her night's assignations while her zootsuited pimp congregated with his fellows in the all-night candy stores to wait for her to return with her night's earnings.

If any of the habitués of the street noticed the weeping blonde girl being led from Number 70, they gave her no more than a passing glance. Too many white girls had run or been dragged from these grimy buildings to cause more than a momentary ripple. Many of them

112

had returned time and again, finally staying to become one of the dead-eyed, shuffling creatures who made it possible for their males to strut their finery, establish their standing in the community.

II.

DONNA ESPIRITO lived in a two-story walk-up in a long row of dun-colored buildings in the Quarter. She led the way up the stairs and leaned against the wall at the top. Her hand still shook so badly she had to give Johnny Liddell the key to open the door.

"I'm scared, Johnny," she told him as soon as the door was closed behind them.

"There's nothing to be scared of, baby," he reassured her.

"But what about her, Angie? They're sure to find her."

"Stop worrying, will you? There's no reason for them to know we were there at all." He patted her shoulder, then looked around the studio apartment. It was furnished with comfortable-looking barrel chairs and a big sofa; the north end was glassed in. "You an artist?"

Donna shrugged. Her eyes were still wide, showed signs of the shock. "That was the excuse I gave my parents for coming to New Orleans to live by myself. I'm not very good."

"Let me be the judge of that." He walked over to the corner where five or six canvases were piled against the wall. He held one up, cocked his head, and studied it critically. "The Cathedral St. Louis?"

114

Donna smiled wanly. "I told you I was no good. If I were, you wouldn't have been able to recognize it." She padded across the room and stood behind him, appraising the painting over his shoulder. "I never was cut out to be an abstractionist. I guess I'm strictly old school."

"I like it," Liddell told her. He set the painting down, went through the other five. "I think the Cathedral one will be my fee."

"You're welcome to it," Donna told him. She walked across the room and dropped onto the couch. "I wish I'd never seen this awful town."

"You can't get rid of trouble by wishing it away, baby," Liddell told her. "Sometimes you can do something about it by facing up to it, dragging it out into the open, and taking it apart." He picked up a paint brush and tested its softness against his palm. "I might be able to help if you'd tell me what it's all about."

The girl sat on the couch, shoulders hunched, staring at the wall.

"What were you doing at Angie's apartment?" Liddell asked.

Donna turned, studied his face. "What were you doing there?" she countered.

"A fair question. I'm investigating Brother Alfred's death. Martinez was close to him. I thought she might be able to—"

"Alfred's death?" It seemed to take a little time to register.

Liddell nodded. "He was found dead this morning in a smashed car. The story's probably in the evening papers. Why?"

The blonde wrung her hands. "Now there's no out. I was hoping Brother Alfred would have mercy, that

115

he'd—" She broke off, stared dry-eyed at the wall, and shook her head miserably.

"You're giving yourself an unnecessary beating, baby," Liddell told her. "Why don't you get it off your chest? Believe me, I'm a big boy. There's very little you could tell me that would make me blush."

"This would."

"Try me."

The girl looked up at him for a moment, then made a decision. She got up from the couch, walked to a small desk, and pulled open a drawer. She extracted a photograph and held it out to Liddell. "What do you think of that?"

Liddell studied the picture and whistled. He held it under the light, examined it. "This isn't a faked picture?"

The girl shook her head, colored.

"How did they ever get you to pose for a picture like that?"

She dropped her eyes. "I don't know. I—I must have been high. I don't remember anything about that night."

Liddell handed the picture back. "Tear it up."

"What good will that do? They have the negative. They made a whole roll of movie film like this."

"They've approached you?"

She nodded. "This morning."

Liddell grinned encouragingly. "Well, you had me worried. If that's all it is, a shake, there's nothing to worry about. I've handled more of those than I like to remember. Let's sit down and work this out."

"There's nothing we can do. If I try anything, they'll send these pictures to my father." She dropped her voice. "It would kill him."

"It won't hurt to talk about it."

116

Donna made a hopeless gesture. "It won't help either. I'm hooked."

"These pictures. Were they taken at the Eye Almighty Temple?"

Donna nodded. "I must have been crazy. But it was—" She fumbled for words, couldn't find them. "Were you ever there?"

Liddell nodded.

"Then you know what I mean. That woman up there on the dais chanting. The beat of the drum. Everybody dancing around growing wilder and wilder. I couldn't help myself. I guess I'm just rotten inside."

"Did you drink or eat anything while you were there?"

"Some wine."

Liddell nodded. "What kind of wine?"

"I don't know. I just remember it was sweet." She looked up at him. "Why?"

He shrugged. "I wouldn't be so hard on myself, if I were you. You were probably drugged. That wine contained either a hypnotic or an aphrodisiac, or both. It's an old trick." He pointed to the picture. "How much do they want for the negative?"

"They don't want money."

Liddell scowled. "What do they want?"

"I guess I passed my screen test." The girl tore the picture bitterly. "They said there are some men that are anxious to meet me. If I do what they say, I'll get the pictures back."

"That's a come-on," Liddell growled. "You'll just be getting in deeper and deeper. You say they called this morning?"

The blonde said, "It was a man. He told me what they expected of me. I'm supposed to see him tonight."

117

"Good. Maybe we can persuade him to be reasonable."

"We?" Her tone indicated that she hardly dared hope.

"Sure. You just hired yourself a boy. You're not keeping that date alone. I'll be around."

She walked up, stood close to him. "There's no price I wouldn't pay you if you'll get those films back for me."

Liddell grinned. "I already set my fee. The Cathedral St. Louis. An original by Donna Espirito. Of the old school."

"Look, Liddell, I'm not trying to put on the wronged virgin act. When I went out there to the temple, I knew it wasn't a pink tea. I went out there for kicks, and I got myself hooked. So if you're doing this to help out a wide-eyed innocent from the parishes, you're being had."

"But?"

She dropped her eyes, massaged the back of her arm. "But I'm no prostitute. I like men, but I like quality in my men, not quantity."

"Look, baby, as long as we're setting the record straight, I'm doing this because I think Brother Alfred's death was caused by a mobster named Marty Kirk. Marty Kirk has a finger in every dirty racket in New Orleans. That includes dope and prostitution. I'll sit in on any game that sounds like it may lead to Kirk. Check?"

"Check."

"Good. Now where are you meeting this character tonight?"

"At the bar in the Café Valentin. It's a club here in the Quarter."

Liddell nodded. "Do you check in with anybody special?"

The blonde shook her head. "He said he'd know me. He saw my picture."

"What time?"

"Ten."

"Good. Don't get there before ten. I'll be sitting at the bar when you walk in. Don't give any sign that you've ever seen me before."

Donna nodded. "All right, if you say so."

"Now, if you'll give me my painting, I'd better get back to my hotel."

The blonde laid her hand on Liddell's arm. "That's hardly a reasonable fee for what you're doing for me."

Liddell reached over and kissed her half-open lips. They were soft, moist. She melted against him, held him close. After a moment, he drew back.

"A deal's a deal, baby. The painting covers the entire fee." He kissed her lips again lightly. "But who knows? I may have to put in an expense account on this job."

Johnny Liddell leaned on the bar at the Café Valentin with the ease born of long experience. The dinner crowd was just beginning to filter in. Already a line was forming on the wrong side of the plush rope that extended across the entrance. Every so often there would be a whispered discussion between the headwaiter and a patron on the wrong side of the rope. Invariably it would be ended by a firm shake of the headwaiter's head.

A four-piece orchestra was playing softly, and a hum of conversation flowed out from the dining room. Inside, the lights were dimmed preliminary to the first floor show of the evening.

Liddell took a swallow out of his glass, glanced down the bar to where Donna Espirito sat tensely on the edge of her bar stool. A muted buzzer sounded behind the bar. The bartender picked up the telephone, muttered into it, nodded, replaced the receiver on its hook.

Then he walked down the bar to where Donna sat,

119

leaned across the bar, and whispered to her. She nodded, threw Liddell a worried look, and started toward an unmarked door near the entrance.

Liddell waited until she had closed the door behind her, finished his drink, then passed a bill to the bartender. When the man behind the bar shuffled off to ring it up, Liddell dropped his cigarette to the floor, ground it out, and headed for the door the blonde had gone through.

A flight of stairs led to a small balcony that overlooked the dance floor below. A young man in a faultlessly tailored tuxedo was leaning on the decorative railing watching the beginning of the floor show below.

"Lost your way?" he smiled pleasantly.

Liddell indicated the closed door. "I want to see the boss."

The man in the tuxedo looked hurt. "Mr. Camden's too busy to see tourists right now." He caught Liddell's arm with a surprisingly strong grip. "You leave your table number with the headwaiter, and if—"

Liddell brought his fist up from the side of his knee, and the man in the tuxedo fielded it with his stomach. The air wheezed out of his lungs like a deflated balloon. His eyes glazed, and a thin stream of saliva ran down his chin. As his knees started to sag, Liddell caught him under the arms, easing him to the floor. He looked over the balcony, saw no indication that the brief scuffle had attracted any attention. He tried the knob on the huge glass door, found that it turned easily in his hand. He slipped his .45 from its shoulder holster, pushed the door open, and stepped in.

The door sighed shut, giving the room that peculiar absence of sound that most soundproofed rooms have.

The first person he saw as he walked in was Gabby

Benton. She was sitting in a big easy chair, legs crossed, a cigarette sending a slow spiral of smoke ceilingward from between her fingers. Her face was pale, her lower lip caught between her teeth.

"Welcome to the party, Liddell," Mike Camden greeted him. He was seated in the mate to Gabby's chair, with his fingers laced across his stomach. "Take Liddell's gun, Sammy."

Liddell felt the snout of a gun ram him in the ribs and made no attempt to resist as the man behind him reached around and relieved him of the .45.

"What are you doing here, Gabby?" Liddell asked.

Gabby shrugged, put the cigarette between her lips, and took a deep drag.

"She's one of them, Liddell. She's part of the gang," Donna Espirito broke in.

"That right, Gabby?" Liddell wanted to know.

Gabby shrugged. "It's like you said, Johnny. You don't get robin's-egg-blue Cadillacs and an apartment on Carondolet off a private detective's salary."

Liddell nodded. "So I did." He turned back to Camden. "You must use a crystal ball. You all acted as though you expected me."

"We find a one-way glass more practical," Camden told him good-naturedly. His voice was silky, smooth with an elusive trace of the Boston Back Bay where he'd gotten his start. His sandy hair had receded from his brow to the crown of his head, exposing a freckled pate. His ready smile plowed white furrows into the mahogany of his cheeks.

Liddell turned, looked at the door he'd come through. From the inside it was transparent, laced with a fine steel mesh. Anyone sitting inside the room could see everything that went on, on the balcony.

"To what do we owe this unexpected pleasure, Liddell?" Camden asked.

"I dropped by to get the negatives and any other prints you may have of those pictures of Donna."

Camden raised his eyebrows. "Did you really!" He pulled a cigarette holder from his pocket, fitted a cigarette to it, and tilted it in the corner of his mouth. "And how did you propose to get them?"

"I intend to take them," Liddell told him.

Camden took the cigarette holder from between his teeth and stared at Liddell for a moment. Then he burst out laughing. "You hear that, Sammy? He intends to take them!"

"He's a real tough guy." The man holding the gun on Liddell grunted. He was a counterpart of the man on the balcony. This edition was a shade shorter, but what he lacked in height, he more than made up in breadth.

"What are you going to do with him, Mike?" Gabby demanded.

Camden pursed his lips, chewed on the stem of the cigarette holder. "I don't know. I think maybe I'll leave that up to Sammy and Lewis."

The man with the gun licked at his lips. "We'll take care of him."

Gabby shook her head. "We can use him."

Camden scowled. "How?"

"That job he did on Lewis out there. That was a real professional job, wasn't it?" she insisted.

Camden nodded. "And Lewis is supposed to be good. What do you think, Sammy?"

The tuxedoed guard growled deep in his chest. "He never could've done it if Lewis expected the joker to jump him."

"But he did do it," Gabby argued. "Look, Mike, this operation can use some muscle like his. Muscle with brains."

"Turn off the pitch, Gabby. Where would I fit in this operation? A bouncer? A Mickey Finn in a tuxedo like this character?"

Sammy swore under his breath and shuffled toward Liddell.

"Hold it, Sammy," Camden snapped. He tapped a quarter inch of ash from the end of his cigarette, flicking off the few specks that settled on his trousers. "All right, Liddell, we're impressed with how tough you are. You interested in a place in the organization? Gabby's right. We can use some muscle with brain." He scowled in the direction of the unconscious man on the balcony. "Muscle we got plenty of."

Liddell seemed unimpressed. "What do you need brains for? To build up a stable of part-time hustlers?"

"Maybe you don't have as much brains as I thought," Camden snapped.

"Wait a minute, Mike," Gabby reached down the side of her chair and brought up a sheaf of papers. "Look, Johnny, this isn't just a nickel and dime operation. Real big shots don't go for pros. They like amateur stuff they don't have to be ashamed to be seen with." She waved the papers. "Here's a list of big shots ripe for plucking. The name of the girl, the name of the guy who hired her, and for how much." She dropped the papers into her lap. "The take in dollars and cents from that end is chicken feed, but the possibilities are unlimited. I can use your help in collections."

"Blackmail?"

Camden shrugged. "Let's say that as a side line we're

in the novelty business. We sell these big shots home-made movies and homemade *tape* recordings. Some of those items come pretty high."

"You can sell out to them, Liddell, but not me," Donna Espirito yelled. "Nobody's dragging me into a filthy racket like that."

Camden turned, studying her impersonally. His right hand whipped upward in an arc and caught her on the side of the face with a sharp crack, sending her reeling backward. Liddell reacted but relaxed when Sammy jabbed the gun's snout into his back.

"One of the first things you learn when you're work-ing for me is not to talk until you're spoken to," Camden drawled. He turned back to Liddell. "It takes time to teach some of these chippies discipline, but they learn."

"Suppose one of them blows the whistle?" Liddell wanted to know.

Camden smiled indulgently. "It's not very likely. Neither they nor the big shots we do business with are in any position to go yelling copper." He held up a reel of film. "Our little friend here wouldn't want certain people to see this film, for instance. She'll do what she's told. They all do."

"I'll bet," Liddell growled.

"What about it, Johnny?" Gabby asked tensely. "Are you in?"

Liddell pinched his nostrils between thumb and fore-finger.

"Don't be a sucker, Johnny," Gabby pleaded. "I know it doesn't smell good at first, but it's here to stay. You might as well get your share."

"What's the matter? Alfred want too big a share for doing the dirty work? That why you and your mob had him killed?"

"We had nothing to do with Alfred's getting himself killed," Camden asserted. "We try to keep killing down in an operation like this. Stirs up too much attention." He took the cigarette holder from between his teeth and examined the thin gray collar of ash at its end. "On the other hand, we can't afford to take chances with a guy who knows too much. So, you're either in or—" He rolled his eyes up from the cigarette, studied Liddell from under lowered lids, and shrugged.

Liddell turned his head, looked at the man holding the gun on him, estimated his chances, and decided they weren't very good. The hand that held the .38 was steady as a rock.

Mike Camden stared at him for a moment, grinning frostily. "Take all the time you want as long as it's made up by the time I get back." He pulled his lanky frame out of the chair, nodding at Sammy. "If he tries anything, burn him. I'll see how Lewis is." He walked across the room, pulled open the glass door, and went out.

"Don't let them do it to me, Liddell," Donna begged in a low voice. "I'd rather kill myself."

"Stop being so melodramatic," Gabby snapped. "From the looks of those pictures, you haven't got too much to lose. Besides, there's as much in it for you as there is for us."

"Five years do a lot of things to a gal like you, don't they, Gabby? Five years and a lot of easy money make a big difference, don't they?"

"Why not? They pass it out for free. Then they scream like they're being murdered when we put them in line to get paid plenty, wear the best clothes, meet the best people, go to the best places for doing the same thing. What's so terrible about that?"

"It's like I said about the city, Gabby. It's amazing that anything that beautiful could hide so much that's rotten."

The man with the gun licked his lips. "You're a real tough guy, Liddell. You mussed up the kid out there. Made him look bad. He's my kid brother." His eyes narrowed. "You heard what the boss said. If you try anything—"

"Cut it out, Sammy. Camden won't like it." Gabby's voice was edged.

"He's got it coming to him. What do we need him for? Me and Lewis can handle all the muscle this operation needs." His finger whitened on the trigger.

"I said cut it out," Gabby snapped. In her hand she held a ridiculously toylike .25. "You're still taking orders from me."

The gunman's eyes swiveled from Liddell to the girl. He swung the gun and snapped a fast shot at her. It hit her shoulder and half swung her around. His second shot caught her squarely, slamming her back against the wall. She pressed her hand to her breast and slid to her knees.

Liddell was on the gunman before he could swing the gun back. He deflected it with his left hand and put every ounce he had into a punch that landed under Sammy's right ear.

The gun fell from the guard's nerveless fingers. Liddell caught him by the shoulder, swung him around, and planted his left to the elbow in Sammy's midsection. Then as the guard toppled forward, Liddell brought up his knee and caught him in the face. There was a dull, crunching sound as the man's nose broke. Liddell chopped down at the other man's neck in a vicious rabbit punch. Sammy hit the floor and didn't move.

126

Liddell crossed the floor to where Gabby sat. Her hand was against her breast in a futile effort to stem the blood that was already seeping through her fingers. Liddell tried to lift her to a chair. She shook her head, managing a semblance of a smile. "Don't move me, Johnny."

Gently, he removed her hand, tore open her blouse, and examined the wound. "You're going to be all right, baby."

Gabby looked past his shoulder at the door. Her fingers dug into his shoulder. "Camden. He's coming back, Johnny."

Liddell glanced toward the glass door. Through it he could see the night-club owner straightening up from an examination of the guard. He looked down with a contemptuous expression, tried to stir the unconscious man with the tip of his shoe. Finally, he gave up in disgust.

Liddell looked around for his gun, then realized he didn't have time to get it. He walked over to the door and waited until Camden's hand had closed over the knob on the other side. Then Liddell yanked the door open suddenly, pulling Camden off balance.

Camden's eyes opened wide when he recognized the private detective. He tried to regain his balance, to go for his gun, but surprise had slowed his reflexes. Before he could get set, Liddell hit him in the stomach with a looping left, followed it with a right to the jaw. Dazed, the night-club owner reeled backward. Liddell was on top of him relentlessly, gave him no chance to get set. Another right to the jaw sent Camden reeling back farther, staggering through the door of the office. The low railing of the balcony caught him in the small of the back, gave way with a screech.

Liddell had a momentary impression of a grin frozen on Camden's face as he disappeared over the side.

From below came a long sustained scream; the orchestra stopped in the middle of a bar. Liddell walked to the edge and looked down.

Mike Camden was spread-eagled over a table. Nearby, a woman in an evening gown seemed transfixed, her clenched fist in her mouth. Her escort pulled her by the arm, rushing her toward the exit. As Liddell watched, the hardier diners started toward the table, congregating morbidly around the body. Near the door, the headwaiter was struggling desperately to get through the crowd that was streaming toward the street.

12.

JOHNNY LIDDELL squirmed uncomfortably on the hard wooden bench in the district attorney's anteroom. He smoked glumly, watching Sergeant Hennessy pace the length and breadth of the office, hands clasped behind his back, chin sunk on his chest.

After what seemed like hours, the door to the corridor burst open, and the district attorney stamped in. He was in a tuxedo, wore a black Homburg, and looked irritated. He nodded briefly at both men, crossed the anteroom with long steps, and flung open the door to his private office.

"All right, sergeant. In here." He tossed a nod in Liddell's direction. "Bring him in with you."

He snapped on the overhead light, tossed his hat at a coat rack, and bustled around behind the desk. Once seated, he looked from the sergeant to Liddell and back. "Well, what was so important that I had to leave right in the middle of a formal dinner?"

Hennessy tugged on the lobe of his ear. "There's been some trouble down in the Quarter, Mr. Wilson."

"How bad?"

"Plenty. Mike Camden's dead."

The district attorney's eyes widened. "Camden? The night-club man?"

Hennessy nodded. "Ran the Café Valentin."

Wilson swore under his breath, swung his eyes in the direction of Liddell, and glowered at him. "Liddell do it?"

The sergeant nodded, looking unhappy.

"I warned you not to pull anything in my town, Liddell." The district attorney slammed the desk with the flat of his hand. "What the hell's he doing wandering around, sergeant? Why isn't he booked?"

Hennessy managed to look unhappier. "It was self-defense, Mr. Wilson. Liddell's partner, the Benton girl's over at Mercy Hospital with a bullet in her lung." He sighed, shook his head. "All hell's going to break loose."

The district attorney subsided and shrank back into his chair. "Suppose you break it down for me?" He looked toward Liddell. "What were you and Benton doing there? Why was she shot?"

"Camden was running a top-drawer vice operation. Liddell stumbled on it. They tried to shut him and his partner up." Hennessy walked to the window and looked down on the darkened streets below. "The whole damn thing is loaded with dynamite."

Wilson continued to stare at Liddell. "Fill it in, Liddell."

"I got a call at the hotel today from a girl. She was in trouble, left word that she had to see me right away," Liddell told him.

The district attorney's eyes jumped to the sergeant.

Hennessy nodded. "We checked the hotel. The clerk read him the message over the phone, then destroyed the message. He doesn't remember the girl's name, but he

130

does remember she wanted Liddell to see her as soon as he got the message."

"Go on," Wilson nodded to Liddell. "Who was the woman?"

"She's a client, and I'd rather not reveal her identity."

The district attorney's face started to turn a brick red, but he controlled it with an effort. "I'm trying to be patient with you, Liddell, but—"

Liddell shrugged. "I'm trying to co-operate with your office, too, Mr. District Attorney, but I don't intend to reveal confidential—"

"You don't intend to!" Wilson roared. He hit the end of his desk a resounding blow with his clenched hand. "I'll have you thrown into the can for so long—"

"You'd better hear the rest of it first, Mr. Wilson," Hennessy told him wearily.

The district attorney dropped back into his chair and glared at Liddell. "All right, go on."

"I'll tell you this much about my client—she comes from a highly respectable family out near Baton Rouge. She started running around with a wild crowd, ended up by going out to the Eye Almighty Temple one night." He paused, fished a cigarette from his pocket, and stuck it between his lips where it waggled when he talked. "That's Brother Alfred's setup over in San Vincente."

The district attorney nodded impatiently, fumbling nervously with the wing of his tie.

"I don't know if you know what goes on out there?" Liddell asked.

"It's out of our jurisdiction," Wilson grunted.

"Well, I can tell you this. They stage some of the God-damnedest orgies out there I've ever seen. My guess is that they spike their wine with either an aphrodisiac or hashish or both. Anyway, the night my client went out

131

to the temple, she was tricked into posing for some pretty lewd pictures. A couple of days later, she got a call from one of Camden's goons telling her how she could buy them back."

Wilson grabbed a fat Havana from his humidor, sank his teeth into it. "How?"

"By services rendered."

The district attorney snorted. "Compulsory prostitution? What are you giving me? That went out with the hoop skirt!"

"Well, then, it's come back with the Bikini. That's the deal."

Wilson glared at him. "Why do they have to go out recruiting new girls? They can get all the girls they want from the back country without any pressure."

"The prostitution aspect of it is only a small phase of the operation." Hennessy walked back to the desk, stood with his hands sunk in his pockets. "It was a prop for the damnedest blackmail setup you ever heard of. He needed girls like this one to attract the big shots he wanted to get."

Liddell nodded. "It's a new type of vice operation, Mr. District Attorney. No pros. Café-society gals you don't have to be ashamed to be seen with. Hell, with the hold Camden and his boys had over half the women in this town through the temple, he could deliver anything from a dowager to a deb. And he had the enforcers to make it stick."

Wilson rolled the cold cigar from one corner of his mouth to the other. "This girl told you all this?"

"Some of it. The rest I filled in for myself."

"What did she call you for? Why not the police?"

Liddell sighed. "She didn't want those pictures to get

132

to her father. She was afraid it would kill him. She wanted me to get them back for her."

"How?"

"She left that up to me."

Wilson snorted, then turned his eyes to Hennessy. "Any proof at all to this wild tale?"

Hennessy nodded. He walked out to the anteroom, came back with a bulging manila folder. "Here's just a sample of the stuff we took out of Camden's files." He flicked his finger through the stacks of pictures, lists of prominent clients. "Some of the names on those lists would make your hair curl."

The district attorney looked up, annoyed. "My hair is already curled."

Hennessy belatedly recalled Wilson's sensitivity over the kinkiness of his hair. "Just an expression," the sergeant grumbled.

Wilson picked up a list, let his eyes run down the names, and his face dropped. He looked up at the homicide man, who nodded sadly. "All top drawer."

"There's enough here to blow the lid right off this town." The district attorney nodded. "Where did they ever get pictures like these? Certainly these men never went out to the temple."

"Some of them did. The rest were set up by girls who were buying their own pictures back from Camden the hard way."

Liddell nodded. "Camden told me he did a land-office business in homemade recordings and homemade movies." He waved at the pile of pictures on the desk. "He had enough on most of those people to hang them."

Wilson pulled a handkerchief from his breast pocket,

patted his forehead. "We'd better contact the Federal Building. We can't move in on that temple, but—"

Hennessy nodded. "I already dumped what we had into their laps. They were trying to get a judge out of bed to get the necessary papers to take the place apart when I left."

Wilson swabbed the side of his neck and replaced the handkerchief. "To get back to Mike Camden." The district attorney looked unhappy now. "I'm going to have to answer a lot of questions in the morning. I'd better have some answers to give." He crushed his teeth into the end of the cigar. "Give me the rest of what happened there tonight."

"Well, when this stooge of Camden's called my client, they told her to show up at the bar in the Café Valentin tonight. When they were ready for her, they'd send for her." He took a last deep drag on his cigarette, blew it ceilingward, and snubbed it out. "I told her to keep the date. I planned to be there when the action started."

The district attorney waged a valiant effort to keep his eyes from straying to the pile of documents on the desk, but lost. He rolled his cigar between thumb and forefinger in the center of his mouth and nodded. "Get to the part about Camden being killed."

"When they sent for the girl to go up to Camden's office, I followed. I wasn't as cute as I thought I was. Mike has a one-way glass door and was waiting for me."

"It was self-defense, Mr. Wilson," Hennessy put in. "Camden's goons tried to take Liddell, but his partner showed up with a cap pistol. One of them pegged a shot at her and got her with the big one. But she'd managed to keep them busy just long enough for Liddell to take over. That was the way it went, Liddell?"

The private detective nodded. "Just about."

"You still haven't told me what happened to Camden," Wilson pointed out peevishly. "What was he doing while all this hassle was going on?"

Hennessy grunted. "Camden went over the side of that balcony outside his office and landed in some dame's demitasse."

The district attorney pulled the cigar from between his teeth and examined the crushed, soggy end. "You think you got all his records?" He didn't look up.

Liddell nodded. "I'm sure of it. The blackmail end of the operation belonged to Camden. The dope-pushing belonged to Brother Alfred. As soon as I find the other links in the chain, I'll pass them along to you."

Wilson tossed his cigar at the waste basket, looked up. "I guess we owe you a vote of thanks, Liddell. With all this, we ought to be able to clean up this vice mess with a minimum of damage to everybody concerned." He scooped up the records and pictures and dumped them back into the Manila envelope. "I hope we can depend on your discretion in this matter, Liddell?"

Liddell grinned crookedly. "I never divulge information of a confidential nature. Not even the name of a client."

The district attorney stood up and extended his hand. "We'll consider that a fair trade."

Liddell pulled himself out of his chair and shook hands. "Mind if I use your phone?"

The district attorney shook his head and motioned to the instrument. "By all means."

Liddell lifted the receiver off its hook, dialed a number, and waited. The receiver buzzed, then, "Mercy Hospital," it intoned.

"I'm inquiring about the condition of Miss Benton. She was brought in this evening. Gunshot wound."

135

"Her condition is satisfactory. She is resting," the receiver told him laconically.

"Has she recovered consciousness?"

"We can't give out that information, sir."

"Just a minute," Liddell growled at the mouthpiece. He shoved the instrument at Hennessy. "Throw your weight around, will you, sergeant? They won't give me any information at all except what day it is."

Hennessy took the phone, held it to his ear. "This is Sergeant Hennessy in Homicide. Who's on with Miss Benton, nurse?"

"Dr. Steckler, sergeant."

Hennessy nodded. "Good. Connect me with him."

The line went dead for a second. "Just a minute, Dr. Steckler's coming on." There was a click, then a man's voice. "Steckler."

"Julius, this is Hennessy down at headquarters. I'm interested in that Benton girl they brought in tonight. The gunshot wound."

"Yeah. It's a pretty rough one, sarge. She hasn't recovered consciousness yet. We've got her on critical."

"When do you expect to have some idea of how she'll do?"

The receiver shrugged. "Hard to tell. We'll keep her under sedatives at least until morning. She's getting infusions now." He hesitated for a moment. "I can give you a call the minute there's any change in her condition one way or the other."

"No. Don't call me. Call Mr. Liddell at—" He held his hand over the mouthpiece. "You still staying at that riding academy on Bourbon?" Liddell nodded, and the sergeant took his hand off the mouthpiece. "Call Liddell at the Hotel Delcort."

"O.K., sergeant." The interne dropped the receiver on

its hook and broke the connection. Hennessy tossed his instrument on its cradle.

"How is she?" the district attorney wanted to know.

"No change. She's still unconscious." He looked over to Liddell. "They're going to keep her quiet at least until morning. After all, she did lose a lot of blood. The rest will do her a lot of good."

Liddell nodded. "Thanks for putting in the fix on the bulletins."

"Glad to." Hennessy watched Liddell glumly. "I've got a squad car out front. Give you a lift back to your hotel if you like."

Liddell looked out the window and shook his head. "I think I'll walk." He flipped a cigarette into his mouth and touched a match to it. "It looks like it's finally cooled off out there."

13.

DONNA ESPIRITO was sitting in the back booth of a street-corner bar near her apartment. She waved Liddell down as he stood in the doorway, squinting through the slowly swirling smoke. He nodded to her, shouldered himself to a place at the bar, and ordered a straight bourbon.

The bartender spilled an ounce into an oversized shot glass, shoved it across the bar. Liddell pushed it back.

"Better make it a double. I want to be able to taste it."

The man behind the bar grunted, tilted the bottle over the glass again, and filled it to the etched white line. He dug under the bar, came up with a handful of ice, a highball glass. He drenched the ice down with a flat soda and spun it across the bar. "One thirty," he told Liddell. He had difficulty with his upper denture when he talked.

Liddell dropped a bill and two quarters on the bar. "I'm going to be sitting in the rear booth back there. In about three minutes send another one over."

The bartender picked up the bill and change, rang it up. He held the two dimes in his hand, looked at Liddell, who nodded. The bartender dropped the two dimes

138

into a glass alongside the register and shuffled off to the other end of the bar.

Liddell turned around, leaned his elbows on the bar, looked the place over. He kept his eyes on the door, waited a few minutes before he picked up his glass, then walked to the rear booth.

"What was that all about?" the blonde wanted to know as he slid in opposite her. "I thought you were passing me by."

"Not a chance, baby. I just wanted to be sure the D.A. didn't slap a tail on me when I left."

"How did everything go?" Donna wanted to know breathlessly.

"Smooth as silk. You're out of the investigation completely." He took a deep swallow and set his glass down. "What are you drinking?"

"I can't drink tonight, Johnny. It goes down just this far, sticks there." She fumbled in her bag, brought up a cigarette, and put it between her lips with a hand that still shook. "Have you heard from the hospital?"

Liddell found a pack of matches and held a light for the girl. "She's in bad shape. She hasn't regained consciousness."

Donna took a deep drag and let the smoke dribble from between her lips. "I'm awfully sorry. You've known her a long time, haven't you?"

"After tonight, I'm not sure I ever knew her, baby."

"She sure had what it took when the cards were down, Johnny. That goon was going to kill you."

Liddell nodded, drained his glass, and set it down. "Yeah, she took it for me." He scowled down at his glass. "I wonder why. I was upsetting what she'd worked years to get—a connection with a foolproof setup. Even if

Sammy hadn't gotten her, it would have meant the end of all that."

Donna shrugged. "She loved you. Isn't that enough?"

Liddell grinned. "She also loved her powder-blue Cadillac and her apartment on Carondolet and all the other things the money could buy. She was a funny girl, baby. I don't think even she could understand some of the things she did."

A waiter with a white apron tied around his middle · flatfooted over with a double shot of bourbon on a tray. "You call for this, mister?" he wanted to know.

Liddell nodded, lifted it off the tray. He dug into his pocket, came up with two bills, dropped them on the still outstretched tray. The waiter went away.

Donna took the remains of her drink and swirled it around her glass. "I guess it's not very easy to turn down a quick buck when you've always wanted the things that only money can buy."

"That's just the point. Why kick over that setup for a broken-down private eye who can do you no good at all?"

The blonde smiled. "Every so often something comes along that you can't buy with money. You want it so badly that the things you can buy with money and the money itself isn't very important any more." She shrugged. "Maybe that's what happened with her."

"Don't go philosophical on me, baby," Liddell grinned humorlessly. "Gabby was a hep gal. She knew how to keep her business life and her sex life well separated. She wasn't too sentimental to have Angie Martinez killed yesterday afternoon."

The blonde stopped with the cigarette halfway to her lips. "She had Angie killed? Why? How do you know?"

"Martinez was killed because she was getting ready to
140

open up to me. I think the news that Alfred was dead must have made up her mind." He picked the cigarette from between Donna's fingers, took a deep drag. "Gabby's the only one who knew that Angie tried to contact me."

"How do you know that?"

He replaced the cigarette. "The musclehead on the desk at my hotel spilled it. Angie had called three or four times, left an urgent message. When Gabby called, he thought it was Martinez again and told her he had all her messages, that he'd have me go see her as soon as I came in."

"But why should she be killed just because she wanted to see you?"

Liddell raked his fingers through his hair, shook his head. "I've been trying to figure that out since it happened. The only sensible guess I've been able to make is that she knew who killed Alfred, and more important, had the proof."

Donna sighed. "In that case, the killer probably has it by now."

Liddell took a deep swallow from his glass. "I'm not too sure of that, baby." He swirled the liquor around his glass and watched the reflections of the lights in the place blink in its depths. "From the looks of her apartment when I walked in there, it had been ransacked from top to bottom."

"So?"

"So unless the killer found it in practically the last place he looked, he didn't find it." The girl frowned, shook her head.

"I don't follow," she admitted.

"Suppose you're searching a place for something. The minute you find it, you quit. Right?" The girl nodded.

"Then, there'd be some drawers that hadn't been pulled out, or a closet that hadn't been emptied. Or the bed wouldn't have been ripped apart. In other words, there would have been some signs that the search was successful, that they found what they were looking for."

Donna took a drag on the cigarette and stared down at the ash tray as she crushed it out. "Then whatever it was she wanted to give you may still be there?"

"That's my guess."

The blonde wrinkled her brows and plucked at her full upper lip. "But by now it will be gone. Maybe the killer's gone back, maybe—"

Liddell shook his head. "Right after he left, you got there. You were still there when I arrived, and we left just before the cops showed up." He made concentric circles on the table top with the wet bottom of his glass. "The police probably kept a man around most of the evening just as a matter of routine. But by now he should be gone."

"You mean you're going back there?"

Liddell nodded; the girl shuddered.

"I wouldn't go near that place for a million dollars." She laid her hand on his arm. "Why take a chance like that?"

"You probably wouldn't understand it if I explained, and I haven't got the time to do it justice. But just put it down to this. I came here to find a man. I found him, and because I found him he was murdered. Now I intend to find the killer, and when I do, I'll wrap him up in a nice neat little package and drop him into the D.A.'s lap."

"You're right."

Liddell's eyes widened. "Most women wouldn't under—"

142

"I didn't mean that I agree with you. I meant you're right. I don't understand it at all."

Marseilles Road in Little San Juan still showed signs of life at two in the morning. A few drunks, white and black, weaved down the street. Some sat on the steps, head sunk below their knees; others snored in vestibules and hallways. A yellow-faced girl in a bright red dress perked up as Liddell swung onto Marseilles, and fell into step beside him. She whispered to him suggestively, tugging at his sleeve. Liddell grinned, shook his head.

The girl lost interest and fell behind.

Liddell walked past Number 70 slowly, looked in all directions for some evidence of a policeman on duty, then was satisfied that Hennessy had left no one to keep an eye on the premises. He turned around, ambled back, and walked up the three steps to the vestibule.

He waited until his eyes had become adjusted to the darkness, then felt his way cautiously to the stairs. Slowly, he climbed the flight to the upper hall, paused at the head of the stairs, and listened. There was no sound but the steady breathing of a sleeping house.

Liddell walked softly to the door of the front apartment, fished out the strip of celluloid, and slid it into the jamb of the door. After a moment, he was able to turn the knob and walk in.

The smell of death still hung over the apartment. He stood against the door, listening for a moment. Then, taking a match from his pocket, he scratched it and took his bearings. The room was just as he had left it that afternoon. The piles of papers and clothing on the floor showed signs of having been examined, but nothing had been removed. He crossed the room to the bedroom.

The bed still held the dingy linen with an ugly brown

143

stain. No attempt had been made to clean the spot on the floor where Angie Martinez had bled to death. The match flickered down to his finger tips, burning him. He dropped it, swearing. He decided to risk a light with the drawn shades.

Methodically he set about searching every inch of the flat. He pulled the drawers out, dug his hand into the recesses, turned them upside down to be certain nothing was attached to their undersides. He stood on his tiptoes and probed into the corners of the shelves on top of the closets. He examined the molding around the room and went over the furniture inch by inch.

The tank on the toilet was equally disappointing. Ready to call it a day, he got down on his knees, examined the sink in the bathroom. Attached to the underside by strips of adhesive tape was a thin alligator wallet. He tore it loose and flipped it open. There were papers in the compartments. He started to finger through the papers, flipping through the cards in it.

There was a screech of tires from the street below. The sound of a car door being opened. Liddell snapped off the light and crossed to the window. Down below was the familiar white and green of a police squad car. Two uniformed policemen were piling out of the car, running for the front steps. Liddell dropped the corner of the shade and sprinted for the hall door.

As he closed the door behind him, he could hear the heavy steps of the cops on the staircase below. He melted into the shadows, started up the stairs to the flight above, two steps at a time.

Behind him he could hear the running steps of the police, the opening and slamming of doors. Liddell cleared the third floor landing just as the policemen started banging on the door he just left. He headed for

144

the rear of the landing where a short stair led to a door that opened onto the roof. He pushed through and closed the door after him. There was a chair standing there. He propped it under the doorknob of the roof door and wedged it shut. Then he ran for the next roof.

The next two houses were uniform and joined, the third was separated by a six-foot chasm. Liddell tried the roof door of the last house, found it bolted from the inside. Desperately he looked around for some way down, spotted a large plank. He dragged it to the edge of the roof, bridged the chasm to the next roof.

Behind him he could hear the shouted curses and instructions as the cops tried to break open the door to the roof. From below came the shrieking of brakes as other squad cars pulled up to join in the search. The perspiration formed in the hollow of Liddell's shoulders, ran down his back in rivulets.

He tested his weight on the plank, tried to avert his eyes from the three-story drop below. He crossed quickly and jumped onto the other roof.

There was a growing hubbub as the residents of Marseilles Road were dragged from their beds by the shrieking cars, the police whistles, the noise of running feet and smashing doors.

Liddell pulled the plank after him to cut off access. Behind him, the roof door at Number 70 gave way with a smash as the policemen managed to batter it from its hinges. They stood on the roof, their flashlights stabbing fingers of light in all directions. Liddell could hear the shouted commands as other cops joined them on the roof, joined the search.

Liddell flattened himself against the roof he was on, wormed his way to the rickety penthouse that housed the stairs. His palms were wet; he could feel the perspiration beading on his forehead, running down into his eyes. When he reached the door, he took a deep breath, prayed that no night lock or bolt would hold it fast. He reached up, grabbed the doorknob, tugged. The door swung open.

He slid through it, closed it behind him, ran down the short stairway to the third-floor landing. Above him, he could hear the cops a couple of roofs away, shouting commands, searching every square inch.

Liddell guided himself along the wall to the staircase. He was halfway down the stairs when the door to the street burst open down below. Flashlights played up the stairwells, there was a clatter of hard-heeled boots as the cops started to do a floor to floor search. Liddell froze back against the wall, out of the prying range of the flashlights, climbed back to the third floor.

Above he could hear the police on the next roof, separated from the house he was in by a three-story chasm. Below, their comrades were working their way up to where he huddled in the malodorous darkness. He cursed under his breath, tried to estimate his chances of getting back onto the roof and making a run for it, realized he was cornered.

He heard the faint scrape of the door first, then the hiss.

"This way," a low voice with a soft Spanish accent ordered.

He squinted in the darkness, could see the dim oval of a face up front. He felt his way along the wall, slid through the door.

"Get off your clothes. *Rapido, por Dios!*"

Liddell ripped off his coat and shirt, wrapped his shoulder holster in them, tossed it under a chair. He kicked off his shoes as he crossed the room to the bedroom beyond, tore off his pants, jumped into the bed. In a moment, bare warm flesh squeezed in against him.

The girl reached up, mussed his hair, smeared sticky lips across his face and mouth. Liddell took a deep breath and tried to still the pounding of his heart.

There were heavy footsteps in the hall, then a pounding on the door.

"Open up!" a heavy voice commanded.

The girl slipped out of bed, grabbed up a kimono, padded out to the door. Liddell could hear her open the door, her shrill voice arguing, the heavier voices of the police. Footsteps clattered across the living-room floor, and two cops entered, guns in hand.

"You have no right to break in my house," the girl shrilled at them.

The cops ignored her. "Who's this?" One directed the beam of the flashlight at Liddell.

"*Mi pichonsita.* I his sweetheart," she snapped.

"Shake the rest of the place down, Jake," the cop told his partner. "I'll see the guy." He walked over, pulled the covers back from Liddell, snickered. "How long you been here, mister?"

"A couple of hours. I—"

"See anything of a guy running through here or hiding any place?"

Liddell shook his head.

The cop turned, looked at the girl appreciatively. "You want to watch these hot peppers, mister. You can get burned."

The other cop returned from a check of the other rooms. "Not here, Ed. How the hell could he get across from that other roof? He can't fly. I tell you he's still hiding in Number Seventy."

They stamped across the floor, slammed the hall door

147

behind them. Liddell could hear the sound of their feet going down the stairs, the slam of the hall door. He wiped the perspiration from his face with the back of his hand.

The girl walked over to the window and watched the street from behind the upturned corner of the shade. Liddell gathered up his clothes and started dressing.

"They going, Chiquita?"

The girl turned from the window and nodded. "They leave two men to watch for you." She snapped on a small lamp and stared at him curiously. "You kill somebody?"

Liddell shook his head. "They've got me mixed up with someone else." He got his first good look at the girl. She was small, dark. Her lipstick was smeared all over her mouth, her eyes were big black marbles. She wore a cheap kimono that gaped open in front, exposing her nakedness. "You can't leave now," she pointed out. "They waiting for you."

Liddell nodded. "There must be a back door, isn't there?"

She shrugged. "Through the cellar." She cocked her head. "Why you not want to stay? You don't like me, eh?"

"I'm crazy about you, but I'd better get out of here before they decide to come back." He dug into his pocket, pulled out a roll of bills, peeled off two fives. "That's to show you how much I like you."

She took the two bills, counted them, danced off to the bedroom. In a moment she came back, struggling into a skirt and blouse. "I go with you, show you the way through the back yard. The *policia*," she snapped her fingers, "they never catch you."

14.

THE NOISE sounded like distant thunder, settled down to the sharp chatter of a machine gun. Johnny Liddell groaned, tried to burrow his head under the pillow, but the noise refused to go away. Finally, he reluctantly opened one bleary eye and decided it was only someone trying to knock his door off its hinges. The clock on the table next to his bed said eight o'clock, the rain pelting against his window frame gave no hint whether it was A.M. or P.M.

The pounding on the door showed no signs of abating. Liddell pulled on his pants, slid his feet into slippers, and shuffled to the door.

"O.K., O.K. Keep your pants on," he growled.

He turned the key and pulled open the door.

"That's a fine way to greet an eager young lady paying you a call at your apartment," Donna Espirito grinned at him impishly. This morning she wore her thick blonde hair in a long page boy that cascaded down onto her shoulders. She wore a loose silk peasant blouse that made her look even younger and complemented the color of her eyes. Liddell noticed that most of the lines of strain he had detected in her face the day before had been erased.

149

He groaned, covered his eyes. "Oh, no. Not you."

The girl walked past him into the room and looked around critically. She placed a large paper bag she held in her arm on the table. "I brought some breakfast. Hot coffee, hot crullers."

Liddell pushed the door shut resignedly. "How jolly." He walked over to the coffee table in front of the couch and helped himself to a cigarette. "Now my reputation in this riding academy is really made. They looked at me like I was a cross between a satyr and perpetual motion when I staggered in last night, and now you come waltzing by."

Donna grinned, wrinkled her nose. "Who cares what they think?" She lifted two cardboard containers of coffee and a tissue-wrapped bundle from the bag, set them on the table. "You'll feel better after you have some coffee." She stopped, sniffed, looked around. "What's that smell?"

Liddell grunted, blew a double stream of smoke through his nostrils. "What's it smell like?"

"Well, to tell you the honest truth, it smells like a cut-rate Sadie Thompson."

Liddell bridled. "I don't know about that cut-rate business. She cost me ten bucks."

The blonde set down the coffee, went over to Liddell, and sniffed at him. "It is you. What'd you do, fall in a gallon of fifty-cent passion water?" She pinched her nostrils delicately between her thumb and forefinger. "Penetrating, isn't it?"

"What are you complaining about?" Liddell growled. "I've got to live with it. I've taken so many hot showers in the past couple of hours, my hide's peeling right off." He sniffed, scowled. "If anything, it's getting stronger."

"Where'd you get it?"

"In bed with a Puerto Rican gal," he told her. He took another suck on his cigarette, blew the smoke through the nostrils. "I can't get the damn smell out of my nostrils." He crushed the cigarette in an ash tray.

"Have fun?" Donna wanted to know.

"Where?"

"In bed with the Puerto Rican girl, of course," she snapped.

Liddell grinned. "Believe it or not, I was hiding from the cops."

The blonde's eyes widened, and she started to giggle. "Of course. What a perfect place to hide. Who'd ever think of looking there?"

"The cops did."

The blonde leaned back, howled. "You mean they actually—" She covered her face, laughed until the tears streamed down her face. "You must have made a dignified picture."

"It was better than getting dragged down to headquarters to explain what I was doing in Martinez' apartment." Liddell walked over, selected a container of coffee, gouged out the top.

"You think it was a trap?"

Liddell shrugged. "I was careless. I guess somebody reported lights in the flat. First thing I knew, the whole area was crawling with cops." He tried the coffee, burned his tongue, swore.

"How'd you ever get away?"

He shrugged. "I managed to make the roof, went over a couple of buildings, ducked into the end one. I started down the stairs and almost ran right into the arms of a couple of cops doing a house-to-house check."

Donna whistled soundlessly.

"I was sure I was cooked. Then this little tamale

151

opened her door, told me to hide out under her sheets. By the time the cops came busting in, I looked as though I'd been there all night."

"You smell it, too," Donna told him. She picked up her container of coffee, cupped her palms about it. "So it was a dry run, eh?"

"Not exactly."

"Aside from your romantic exploits, I mean," the blonde told him coldly. "You went up to Angie's to look for something? Remember?"

"That's what I mean."

Donna put down her container. "You mean you found it?"

"Certainly I found it," Liddell grumbled. "That's what I went for."

"What was it?"

Liddell shook his head. "That's where the dry run comes in, baby. It was nothing. A wallet with some papers in it. It didn't make a bit of sense to me."

The blonde's features mirrored her disappointment. "But it must have, Johnny. Angie must have thought it would mean something to you when she called. And certainly the one who killed her thought it was important—"

Liddell shrugged. "I'm not even sure this is what she wanted to show me." He walked over to the closet, fumbled in the breast pocket of his jacket, brought back an alligator wallet, and tossed it on the table. "The guy it belongs to was Puerto Rican. It might have been there when Martinez moved there."

"No, this couldn't have been there more than a few days, Johnny. Here's a ticket stub dated only a couple of days ago." She flipped through the papers, picked out a post-card-sized picture of a half-naked, generously proportioned brunette. She looked it over, whistled. "This look like your alibi?"

Liddell shook his head. "That was in there."

Donna held the picture so she could squint at the inscription. "I can make out her name. Benita. What's the rest of it say?"

"*Quien besabas tu hoy,*" he read. "That's the Spanish equivalent of 'I wonder who's kissing her now.'" He watched while she riffled through the wallet. "There's nothing in it. Belongs to some guy named Ramón Jorges apparently. From the stuff in it, looks like he's a Riqueno. That San Juan ticket stub and the courtesy cards." He shrugged. "Doesn't mean a thing."

The blonde stuffed the papers back into the wallet and tossed it on the table. "Hear from the hospital yet?"

Liddell shook his head. He finished his coffee, crushed the container in his fist, and threw it at a wastebasket. Then he walked over to the phone, lifted it from its cradle. "This is Liddell in three-forty. Got anything down there for me?" He waited while the girl checked. "A letter? Send it up, will you? No calls, though?"

The receiver chattered at him.

"Get me Dr. Steckler at Mercy Hospital, will you?"

He dropped the receiver back on its hook. "No word from the hospital yet." He ran his fingers over the faint stubble on his face. "I figured there would be some word before now."

Donna finished her coffee and dumped it in the bag. "Maybe she's resting, and they don't want to disturb her." She rewrapped the doughnuts, dropped them into the bag with the empty coffee container. She started slightly as the phone jangled.

Liddell picked it up, held it to his ear. "Dr. Steckler?

153

My name's Liddell. Sergeant Hennessy called early this morning—"

The receiver cut him off with a metallic chatter.

"Oh, I see. What are her chances, doc?"

He nodded as the voice on the other end droned on, and scowled at the faded rug.

"I understand. Suppose I get there in an hour or so. Think I can see her for just a minute?" The receiver reassured him. He nodded. "Thanks, doc," he said and hung up the phone.

"How is she?" Donna wanted to know.

Liddell shook his head. "Not good. They kept her under opiates all night. They've been giving her infusions. She doesn't seem to rally the way they think she should."

"Will they let you see her?"

Liddell nodded. "She should be coming out of it in about an hour. The doc says she's been calling for me, working herself up into a state. I guess it would be easier on her if they let me talk to her than to keep her fighting them."

There was a knock on the door. "That's a boy with some letter, Donna. Take it for me, will you? I'm going to get under the shower again and try to scald off this stench."

He closed the bedroom door after him, stepped under a red-hot shower, followed it with a skin-tingling cold shower. He was shrugging into his shirt when Donna knocked on the door.

"Come on in, I'm decent," he called.

She came in with a large Manila envelope in her hand. "I thought you might want to see this. The return address says Federal Bureau of Identification."

Liddell frowned, took the envelope out of her hand, and stared at it for a moment. Then he tore the end open

and dumped the contents on his bed. It consisted of a
B.I. card with a front and profile portrait and a set of
fingerprints and a note. He handed the card to the girl
and unfolded the note. It was dated Washington the day
before and said:

DEAR JOHNNY,
Almost fell off my feet when I got the note from you. I
don't know where you got the prints, but they belong to
a boy we'd like to have some conversation with. As you
can see by the attached, he's Al Frederici. Used to be
a member of Lou Mendel's mob out on the Coast.
Dropped out of sight about five—six years ago. He's
wanted for questioning in a couple of killings out there.
We want him for his activities with the white stuff—
women and powder. If you know where he is, contact
our boy down there, Ben Grayson, at the office in the
Federal Building on South Street. I know Ben would ap-
preciate the information. Drop by the next time you're
passing through.

It was signed "Mel."
Liddell flipped the note down onto the bed, walked
over, and peered at the B.I. card over the blonde's shoulder. The man on the card was round-faced, wore a thin
pencil-line mustache. His eyebrows were bushy, his eyes
set close to the bridge of the thin, pinched nose. He was
almost totally bald.
"Recognize him?" Liddell asked.
The blonde looked up, then studied the card again,
shook her head. "I never saw him before in my life."
"That's what you think. That's the way your pal,
Brother Alfred, looked without all his hocus-pocus
beard." He picked up Mel's note, glanced through it
again. "His real name's Al Frederici. He was a mobster
out on the coast until the F.B.I. ran him underground."

Donna stared hard at the picture, then shook her head. "How many hundred years ago was this picture taken? He didn't look like that at all." .

Liddell selected a tie and knotted it around his neck. "He wasn't supposed to. Don't forget, he was on the lam." He took his shoulder holster from the back of a chair, hung it in his closet, turned the key, and dropped it into his pocket. From his dresser drawer, he took a little snub-nosed .38 and dropped it into his jacket pocket. "One thing's a cinch. They'll never recognize him the way he looks now."

Johnny Liddell left the blonde in a cab in front of Mercy Hospital. As the cab pulled away, he sprinted across the teeming sidewalk and up the steps. He crossed the lobby to a small desk where a nurse in freshly starched uniform presided.

"I'd like to see Miss Benton, nurse. Gabrielle Benton."

The nurse consulted a small filing cabinet, checked a card, looked up. "I'm sorry. Miss Benton can't have any visitors."

"I know. But I was sent for."

"Your name?"

"Liddell. Johnny Liddell. Dr. Steckler asked me to come right out."

The nurse turned the card over, nodded. "Yes, Mr. Liddell, doctor is expecting you." She got up from her desk, led the way to a double glass door, pushed it open, and held it for him. "You follow this corridor to the end, then bear right. The charge nurse's desk is right at the turn. She'll take care of you."

Liddell nodded. His heels clicked loudly against the concrete floor of the corridor. At the far end, he turned to the right, stopped at another desk. The nurse was fat, comfortable, and gray-haired. She smiled at him.

156

"Looking for someone?"

"Miss Benton."

The nurse consulted a sheet in front of her. "You're the Liddell she's been calling for?" She looked him over and smiled. "Can't say I blame her." She waved to a white chair. "Sit down for a minute. Doctor just went in to see her. It won't take long."

Liddell nodded. "How's it look, nurse?"

The gray-haired woman pursed her lips. "She might make it. Stranger things than that have happened. But it would be a miracle." She tucked a stray wisp of white hair under her cap. "We're doing everything we can for her, of course, but she'd lost an awful lot of blood by the time we got her."

Liddell nodded, fished a cigarette from his pocket, and stuck it between his lips. As an afterthought, he pointed to it. "O.K.?"

"Better not if you're going in there."

He nodded, pulled the unlit cigarette from between his lips, tossed it at a sand-filled urn. A door marked 105 opened; a nurse came out wheeling a treatment table.

"They're finishing up now," the gray-haired woman whispered.

Liddell got up just as a thin little man in surgical blues walked out of the room. A sickly sweet odor seemed to flow from the open door.

"This is Mr. Liddell, doctor," the nurse told the little man.

Dr. Steckler looked up from the notes he was making. "Oh. I'm glad you got here, Liddell." He capped his fountain pen and stuck it in his breast pocket. "She's been calling for you again."

"How is she?"

The doctor pursed his lips, shook his head. "Her con-

157

dition is very grave. The bullet penetrated her right lung. There's been a lot of hemorrhaging internally."

"Didn't they get the bullet out?"

Dr. Steckler stuck a badly macerated fingernail between his teeth, chewed at the cuticle. "We couldn't risk going in after it. She's too weak." He consulted the watch on his wrist. "You'd better go in. Don't stay too long."

Liddell nodded. "Sure it's O.K.?"

"You may as well. Until she talks to you she'll be working herself into a state that will probably do her more harm than if you do talk to her."

"You're the doctor."

"Just keep her as quiet as possible. Don't let her get excited."

Liddell turned the knob and walked into 105. Gabby Benton lay propped up on a huge pillow in a white bed. Her blonde hair was piled on top of her head, her face was abnormally white, her lips bloodless. The blue shadows under her eyes were accentuated. She opened her eyes as Liddell walked up, worked on a smile.

"They didn't want to let me talk to you, Johnny. At first, I was afraid you didn't want to talk to me." Her eyes were large, bright.

"You know better than that, baby. It's just that they wanted you to rest so you can get out of here faster."

Gabby closed her eyes, snorted. "Don't kid me, Liddell. I'm a big girl. I know when I've had it." She wet her lips with the tip of her tongue. "How about Mike Camden?"

"Dead."

She opened her eyes, nodded. "The rest of them?"

"In the tank. Look, don't worry about that. It's—"

"I want to know. How about the girl? The little blonde kid?" She stared at him fixedly.

Liddell touched his thumb and forefinger, made a circle. "In the clear. The pictures and films are ashes by now. She got out before Hennessy got there."

Gabby took a long, sighing breath. "You destroyed all Mike's records?"

Liddell shook his head. "No. The D.A. needed them as evidence. Don't worry, he'll go easy on the innocent ones involved. But he needs all the ammunition he can get to smash the vice ring."

"The temple?"

"The Feds moved in on it last night, baby. The whole operation has been smashed."

Gabby looked up at him. "I guess it couldn't last forever, could it, Johnny? How about Marty and Wanda?"

"I don't know. But my guess is they'll have a tough time tying Marty to it. And Wanda'll probably go underground."

The blonde nodded. "You know I was in it, too, Johnny. Up to my neck."

Liddell nodded, patted her shoulder. "That's all in the past, baby. The important thing to worry about now is the future."

"But I want to tell you." She licked at her lips, pleaded with her eyes. "I want you to know."

"All right, baby."

"We checked the financial standing of prospects before we got them out to the temple. We knew how much they were good for, how easy they'd be to put the boots to."

"Don't talk about it, Gabby."

"It was a foolproof setup. We had every angle covered. Marty said there wasn't a chance of a squeal, and now look." She closed her eyes, wagged her head. "Funny how things change. We were riding on top of the world,

159

money was pouring in. Everything was running so smooth—"

Liddell pulled a chair close to the bed. "Then what happened?"

"Alfred disappeared. Marty Kirk started getting the shakes. He wanted me to find Alfred." She shook her head. "I wasn't geared for anything like that. I didn't even know how to go about it."

"So you suggested me."

Gabby nodded. "I didn't mean to drag you into all this mud, Johnny. I thought you'd find Alfred and everything would start running smoothly again."

"Well, Alfred's been found."

A cough racked the girl's shoulders. "But dead. Now the heat's really on Marty."

"Why not? The heat's always on a killer. He should have thought of that before—"

The girl reached out and grabbed Liddell's hand with hers. "Marty Kirk didn't kill Alfred, Johnny. The only way he could bail himself out was to find Alfred alive."

"Why?"

Gabby's breathing became shallower. Liddell reached for the button to summon the nurse, but the girl caught his hand, shook her head. "Let me finish. Marty was handling something for the syndicate. Something big, important. The man he was supposed to contact never showed up, and Alfred disappeared at the same time. Marty thought they were together. With Alfred dead, he'll never find Jorges."

Liddell felt a little prickle between his shoulders. "Who?"

"Jorges. He was the guy Marty was supposed to contact."

"What was the deal?"

160

Gabby shook her head. "That's the rough part of it. Nobody knows. Not even Marty. He got word to contact this Jorges at a certain place and time. Jorges never showed, but the lady who rented the apartment described Alfred as one of his visitors."

"And Marty still doesn't know what the contract was?"

Gabby shook her head. She started coughing violently, turned her face to the wall. "With Alfred dead, Marty takes the full rap for blowing the contract."

Liddell squeezed her hand, pushed the button for the nurse. "Don't talk any more, baby. The nurse will be right here."

She turned back to him, her eyes glittering brightly, two round red spots in her cheeks. "I don't need the nurse." She tightened her grip on his hand. "Kiss me, Johnny."

Liddell leaned over, pressed his lips to her half parted ones. They grew slack, failed to respond.

15.

THE RAIN had turned into a full-fledged downpour by the time Johnny Liddell left the hospital. He ran down the steps, looked in either direction for a cab, saw none, pulled up the collar of his jacket, and started to slosh through the puddles toward Canal.

A man parked in a gray Chevrolet at the curb rolled down his window. "You Liddell?" he called.

Liddell squinted at him but failed to recognize him. "Why?"

The man in the car dipped into his pocket, came up with a leather case, and flipped it open. "My name's Grayson. I'm with the Bureau." He pushed open the door. "I tried to reach you at your hotel, and they told me you might be here. Give you a lift back to your hotel?"

Liddell nodded, slid into the front seat, and closed the door behind him. The F.B.I. man reached up, wiped the fog from the inside of his windshield, and stamped the motor into roaring life.

"How's the girl?" he asked.

"Dead."

Grayson shook his head. "Tough." He slid the car into gear. "Use a drink?"

162

Liddell nodded. "As a starter."

"Any special place?"

"Someplace low down. To match the weather."

Grayson headed the car toward the Quarter. "I know a place. Not very fancy. But they don't bother you, either." He respected Liddell's disinclination to talk, concentrated on pushing the car through the narrow streets. After a few minutes, he pulled up in front of a reproduction of an old-time saloon, authentic down to the swinging doors.

The barroom had sawdust on the floor, little tables scattered in organized confusion. A man in his shirt sleeves behind the bar waved to Grayson as he came in. He left the two customers at the far end of the bar, walked down to greet the newcomers.

"Hi, pal." He wiped his hands on his apron, pushed a red paw across the bar at the F.B.I. man. "You don't get around much any more."

"Meet Johnny Liddell from New York. Conch here's a retired bootlegger, Johnny. Although from the taste of some of the stuff he pours off that back bar, I'm not too sure about the retired part."

The man behind the bar grinned. "You know I never pour you nothing but the best, pal." He extended the red hand again, gave Liddell a firm squeeze. "Glad to see you, pal. Come around any time you're in the Quarter." He looked to Grayson. "What'll it be?"

"You're not using the back room, are you, Conch?" asked Grayson.

The bartender shook his head. "Help yourself."

"What do you drink, Liddell?" Grayson wanted to know.

"Bourbon."

The bartender reached back to the back bar, selected

a bottle, put it on a tray, added some ice and water. "Anything else, pal?"

Grayson shook his head, picked up the tray, led the way to a door next to a bank of phone booths in the rear. He pushed the door open with his foot, set the tray down on the table.

Liddell followed him in, kicked the door shut. He put down his jacket collar, wiped some rain off his shoulders. Grayson picked up the bottle, split the seal around the top with his thumb nail.

"You get a letter from Mel Marks in our home office this morning?" he asked.

Liddell nodded. "Just before I left."

Grayson tilted the bottle over each of the glasses, poured in a stiff peg, and set the bottle down. "He sent me a copy of the stuff. Looks like you stumbled across someone the Bureau would like to talk to."

Liddell picked up his glass, dropped some ice cubes into it, and swirled the liquor around over the ice. "It'd be a good trick if you could do it. He's dead."

Disappointment shadowed the F.B.I. man's eyes. "Well, at least now we know where he is." He turned a chair around, straddled it. "All I've got to do then is verify the make and we can close his file for good." He picked up his glass, took a swallow. "Where is he?"

"San Vincente parish morgue. But you're not going to be able to verify those prints there."

"Why not?"

"He was burned to a crisp in a phony auto accident. At least, I'm convinced it was a phony, but I can't prove it."

Grayson scowled at him. "But you got his prints. Where'd you get the ones you sent to the Bureau for a check?"

"In his private bathroom over at the Eye Almighty Temple. Your boy called himself Brother Alfred."

The F.B.I. man clapped his palm to his forehead. "Oh, not him. Some of our boys knocked over that phony temple of his last night."

Liddell nodded. "That's the guy."

"Then we've really got trouble, Liddell." He pulled a pipe from one pocket, a tobacco pouch from another. "Brother Alfred's body was released for burial yesterday. He's not in the morgue over there. He's buried."

"Who claimed him?"

The F.B.I. man dug the bowl of his pipe into the pouch, started packing it with the tip of his index finger. "Nobody, far as I remember. It was a potter's field job." He jammed the pipe between his teeth, chewed on the stem. "That complicates things. Now I've got to go through channels, get a writ, get him dug up, try to match the prints."

Liddell emptied his glass, set it down. "Be a waste of time. There's nothing left of his hands."

Grayson scratched a wooden match, held it to the bowl of the pipe, sucked noisily. "You'd be surprised what they can do these days." He dug into his pocket, brought out a copy of the B.I. card identical to the one that had been sent to Liddell. "That's about our only hope for clinching the identification."

Liddell nodded. "There wasn't enough left of his face to recognize. His glasses were smashed, and—"

"Glasses?" Grayson studied the card, scowled. "He had twenty-twenty vision back in 1947 according to this. What makes you think he wore glasses?"

Liddell shrugged. "I saw them on him." He caught the bourbon bottle by the neck, tilted it over his glass.

165

"Could have been part of his disguise. They were probably plain window glass."

Liddell shook his head. "They were real thick. Showed a pretty strong correction." He set the glass down, held his hand out for the B.I. card. "Can I take a look at that?"

Grayson passed it over, watched the private detective read it word for word. When he finished, he glowered at the card, flipped it at the table. "I'm beginning to get a funny feeling about this case, Grayson." He fished in his pocket, brought up a cigarette.

The F.B.I. man watched him. "About what?"

"A lot of things that don't fit. But you know what? They'd all begin to fit together if it turned out that that body in that car wasn't Alfred's at all."

Grayson sucked on his pipe, blew a heavy fog of smoke toward the ceiling, considered it. Then he shook his head. "That's pretty far-fetched. It was his car. There were plenty of his personal belongings in it, the usual identifiable material. They even got a make from some girl that worked with him."

"It could all have been staged."

"If it didn't belong to Alfred, whose body was that in the car?" The F.B.I. man blew a string of smoke rings at the ceiling, watched them spread and disintegrate.

Liddell shrugged. "I might make a guess, but it would be strictly a guess." He set his cigarette on the corner of the table, leaned back. "It would explain a lot of things that don't make sense otherwise." He picked up his glass and took a deep swallow. "Where did they bury the body?"

"I don't know. I could probably find out. Why?"

"I just want to satisfy my curiosity."

Grayson scowled at him. "You wouldn't be thinking of digging him up?"

Liddell shrugged. "It's been done before. By digging him up maybe I can save someone else from being in the same spot he's in. Namely me."

The F.B.I. man rattled the stem of his pipe against his teeth. "What a blessing to be deaf. In that way I can't hear illegal proposals."

"Mel told me you'd co-operate. All I want to know is where they buried Alfred. You don't have to know why."

Grayson nodded. "O.K." He walked to the door, stopped with his hand on the knob. "I suppose you know that if you're caught you couldn't get licensed as a dog catcher in any state of the Union?"

"You were going to get me some information, remember?"

The F.B.I man nodded. "I know I'm going to hate myself for this in the morning, but a deal's a deal."

The sedan hummed over the road leading to San Vincente. The rain lashed furiously at the closed windows of the car, sending streams of water cascading down the windshield. Johnny Liddell squinted through his window at a road sign as it flashed past.

"The parish cemetery is five miles ahead," he told Grayson. "How we going to do this? We can't walk in the front gate with a couple of shovels on our shoulder and start digging. Besides, how do we go about finding his grave?"

"See, and you didn't want me to come along!" Grayson grinned. "I've got it all figured out. Up about a mile or so, there's a back road that runs behind the cemetery." He peered out through the inverted V cut by the windshield wiper. "I don't think we have to worry about any watchmen prowling around in this weather. If there is a

167

watchman, he'll probably stick close to his shanty up front."

Liddell subsided and watched the scenery flit by his window. After a few miles, Grayson skidded the car off the macadam onto a dirt road. A few minutes later, Liddell could make out the shapes of tombstones and shafts.

"Here's the cemetery," he pointed out to Grayson.

The F.B.I. man shook his head. "That's the private section. Potter's field is farther down." He pulled a folded paper from his pocket and passed it to Liddell. "The office says Alfred was buried in Section Seven. See if you can tell from that map where Section Seven is."

Liddell flattened the map out on his lap, studied it, and stabbed with a stubby forefinger. "There it is. Not too far back off the road." He traced back to the black line representing the macadam road. "It's about a mile in from the beginning of the cemetery on this road."

The car swayed along for another half mile, then Grayson pulled the car off the road under a big tree, cut the motor.

"We're about opposite Section Seven," Grayson guessed. "Alfred's grave can't be much more than a hundred and fifty feet or so from here." He got out of the car, walked around to the trunk. Liddell could hear the clatter of shovels.

"Look, we won't have to do any digging. Down here they bury them above the ground," Liddell told him.

Grayson grunted. "Not in potter's field. That's for the elite." He shouldered a shovel and held one out to Liddell. Then he crossed the road and led the way through the high weeds to the low wall that enclosed the rear of the cemetery. They tossed the shovels over one at a time.

Liddell laced his fingers, made a stirrup, boosted
168

Grayson over. In a matter of seconds he, too, straddled the wall, dropped to the other side.

"This way," Grayson muttered. "Alfred was probably the last one in, so we'll hit for the freshest grave."

They walked past low mounds to the end of the plot where fresh earth marked a newly turned grave. "This must be it." He dropped his shovel. "We'd better tackle it in relays."

"How far is the watchman's shanty from here?" Liddell wiped the rain from his face, looked around.

"At the entrance to the private section. That's a couple of miles from here. You start the digging, I'll keep my eye peeled."

Liddell picked up his shovel. "I sure hope to hell this is worth the trouble." He stepped on the new grave, his shoes sinking in the soft loam. The shovel bit into the dirt.

He was knee deep in a six-foot hole when Grayson spelled him. The F.B.I. man worked steadily for ten minutes and was breathing heavily when Liddell took over again.

They had been at work about forty minutes when Johnny Liddell's shovel scraped on wood. He stopped, tapped with his shovel. "Hit it."

Grayson jumped down into the hole with him. "We'll have to clear enough room to pull the whole box out. We can't work down here. You take a rest topside. I'll get in a few licks. When I yell, drop me the hooks, and I'll get it set to pull out."

It took another ten minutes to clear enough space around the pine casket to attach hooks to the sides. Grayson tossed the ropes up to Liddell, then clambered out. "O.K., let's pull her up to the level and slide her out," he panted.

169

But it took fifteen minutes of grunting, swearing, and sweating before the plain box finally slid out onto the ground. Johnny Liddell wiped the beaded moisture from his face, leaned weakly against the coffin, and panted.

"And I'm the guy that was going to come out here and tackle this alone. What's next, boss?"

Grayson pulled a nearly full bottle of bourbon from his jacket pocket, passed it over to Liddell. "I lifted this from Conch in case of an emergency, and there'll never be a greater one."

They each took a deep swallow from the bottle, recapped it, laid it down on the ground. Grayson took his shovel, inserted the tip of it under the lid of the coffin, used it as a lever. The lid creaked complainingly as it was forced open. A hot, dry odor of decay rose from the interior.

"That does it," Liddell said huskily. He was glad of the warm glow that the liquor had left in his stomach.

Grayson pushed the cover of the casket aside, looked in, whistled soundlessly. "You're right about one thing. There's not much of him left to work on. Now what's this hunch of yours?"

Liddell stepped beside him, bent over the box. "Let's see that B.I. card again, will you, Grayson?"

Grayson handed him the card, watched curiously while Liddell took a pencil from his pocket, pushed down on the front teeth of the thing in the box. "That's not Frederici in there any more than it's me," he growled.

"How do you know?"

Liddell jabbed the card at him. "Frederici had his two front teeth on a removable bridge. This guy still has his own. Your pal Frederici is still among the living, and I've got a client I owe an apology to."

Grayson examined the teeth of the corpse, then straightened up. "You stay here until I can get to a phone and get an exhumation order, Liddell. I don't know who this is, but he's certainly not Al Frederici."

"You want me to stay here alone in this rain?" Liddell growled.

"Stop moaning, will you?" The rain dripped off Grayson's nose and' chin, made mud of the patches of clay that stuck to his suit. He pointed to the bourbon bottle. "You've got Old Granddad there to keep you company."

"That's different," Liddell nodded.

16.

THE CLERK behind the ornate desk in the lobby of the Carter Apartments raised his heavy-lidded eyes from a contemplation of the carnation in his buttonhole. He flattened the hair over his right ear against his head with a hand decorated with a heavy gold identification bracelet. He waited for Liddell to speak first.

"Tell Marty Kirk that Johnny Liddell wants to see him," Liddell snapped. He didn't wait for an answer, headed for the bank of elevators. He gave no sign that he had caught the signal that passed between the clerk and the sleepy-eyed man on the couch.

Tim ambled up behind Liddell as he entered the elevator marked "Penthouse," nodded to the operator. "Hello, Liddell." He held his hand out.

Liddell slipped the .45 from its shoulder holster, dropped it into the sleepy-eyed man's hand.

"Carrying Big Bertha today, eh?" He eyed the gun critically. "Don't see why anyone uses a cannon like this. Guy that knows what he's doing can do as much damage with a twenty-two."

"Maybe when I squeeze a trigger I like to see the guy I'm shooting at go down," Liddell growled. "I've seen them stand and argue with a lot more iron than a twenty-

172

two in them. When this baby hits them, they stay hit."

"I'll still take the twenty-two," Tim drawled. He stayed on the elevator when it reached the penthouse, and rode down with the operator.

The pretty boy with the wavy hair and the blue flannel suit was draped at the desk in the outer room. He looked up as Liddell walked toward him, then dropped his eyes back to a contemplation of his nails.

"If you weren't in such a hurry, the clerk could've told you Marty isn't seeing anybody today, shamus. You took the ride for nothing."

Liddell started to walk past the desk toward the door to the apartment. The man in the blue suit stuck his leg across the doorway.

"You don't hear so good, do you, peeper?" Leo didn't lift his eyes. "Go on back to your keyhole peeping or you won't look so good either."

Liddell stopped at the outstretched leg, looked down at it. "Get it out of the way before I break it off," he told him in a deceptively mild voice.

Leo looked up, then pulled back the leg. He pulled himself to his feet. "I'm sorry, sir," he bowed sarcastically, "I didn't know you wanted to pass." He feinted a pass at Liddell's stomach. When Liddell instinctively covered up, he found his arm caught in a lock. He had the sensation of flying through the air, hit the wall with a thud, and slid to a sitting position on the floor.

The man in the blue suit walked past him, punched at the elevator button. "Always glad to see you, shamus. I don't get enough exercise these days." He kept his finger on the bell.

Liddell shook his head, cleared the fuzziness, got to his feet. Leo grinned at him, faked a sigh. "Don't tell me you want more." He came toward him on the balls of his

173

feet, arms swinging low. "I've been told to give a guest anything he wants."

He swung lightly at Liddell's face with his left, chuckled when the private detective moved his head far enough for it to pass over his shoulder. With perfect co-ordination the guard followed up with a right hook to the stomach. Liddell fielded it with his arm, circled to the right, threw a left and right into Leo's face, knocking his head back.

The grin faded from the guard's face; he moved in, pumping lefts and rights at Liddell. Instead of falling back, the private detective planted his feet, put everything he had into a left and right to the other man's midsection. Leo's face went purple, he folded up over his folded hands and stumbled. Liddell stepped back, brought his right up in a stiff, looping uppercut. Leo's carefully shellacked hair flew straight out. He went backward, and sat down hard.

The man in the blue suit was no longer dapper. His thin purple lips were now blue, his eyes watery. His carefully combed hair hung down over his face. His head rolled uncontrollably from side to side on the top of his body. Liddell walked over, picked him up by the lapels, dragged him to his chair. He had lost all interest in his surroundings.

Liddell turned the knob, pushed the door open, walked in. A girl looked up from where she leaned against the piano. She was tall, full blown. Her thick blue black hair was piled on top of her head; a green sweater was charged with the thankless task of restraining her full bosom. Her lips were full, tantalizing. Liddell could feel the impact of her eyes across the room.

He stared at her for a moment, tried to understand

174

why she looked so familiar. Then it came to him—but the last time he had seen her she wore shapeless red robes, no make-up, and her hair tumbled over her shoulders.

She returned his stare. "How did you get in here?"

"The door was open—Wanda," he told her.

"What about Leo?"

Liddell opened the door, pulled Leo up from his chair. "He knocked himself out making me feel welcome." He released his hold, and Leo dropped back into his chair like a sack of wheat. Liddell re-entered the living room, closed the door behind him. "Where's Marty?"

She inclined her head toward an inner room. "He'll be right out." She walked toward where he stood. She still gave the illusion of gliding, but it was more spectacular to watch than when she had worn the shapeless robes. She stopped alongside Liddell, turned the full impact of her eyes on him. "That night at the temple—I had the feeling we'd meet again." She smiled lazily. He could smell her perfume—heavy, disturbing. Her lips gleamed softly, moistly. "I'd better see if I can get some help for Leo. It looks as though you've about ruined him." As she walked past, her full hips worked easily, tantalizingly against the tight-fitting skirt. It didn't take a detective to deduce that she wore nothing under it.

After the door had closed after her, Liddell walked over to the oversized couch, picked up a copy of *Life* from the coffee table, glanced through it. A door opened and closed off to the left.

Marty Kirk stood in the doorway. At his side, the little man named Hook stood, hand sunken in jacket pocket.

"How did you get past Leo?" Marty growled.

175

"I just went all through that with Wanda," Liddell grunted. "We tried to prove to each other how tough we were. He wasn't."

"What do you want?" Kirk's voice was edged with something more than irritation. "What are you doing here? You here for your pay-off?"

Liddell shook his head. "I didn't do the job." He dropped the magazine onto the coffee table. "Al Frederici is still alive."

Kirk's jaw dropped. "What are you talking about?" he demanded.

"Have it your way," Liddell shrugged. "Brother Alfred is still among the living. That make any more sense?"

Kirk crossed the room to where two cut-glass decanters sat on a small silver platform. He poured a stiff drink into a glass, tossed it off. "You'd better get on the door, Hook. Nobody gets in here. Understand? Nobody."

Hook nodded, crossed to the door, opened it, and went out.

"Now start talking, shamus," Kirk snarled. "What about Frederici?"

"The guy in the car wasn't Al," Liddell told him with a shrug. "It must have been Jorges."

Kirk had to put a hand out against the wall to steady himself. "Then Frederici killed him." He wiped his mouth with a shaking hand, tried to pull himself together. He tottered over to the couch and dropped into it. "You know about Jorges, then?"

Liddell shook his head. "I just know that Jorges disappeared about the same time as Alfred. Who was he?"

Kirk dropped his face into his hands, shook his head. "He was on some kind of a job for the big boys. They didn't spill what it was. They just wanted me to keep my

176

eye on him." He dropped his voice. "He had over a half a million dollars belonging to the syndicate." He looked up. "I was supposed to make sure nothing happened to him."

Liddell whistled soundlessly. "What was the dough for?"

"I don't know. It was none of my business. It came from the big boys." He got up, paced the room. "Frederici must be trying to highjack it." He stopped, swung back to Liddell. "There's a twenty-five-thousand-dollar bonus in it for you if you turn him up now. What do you say?"

Liddell shrugged. "I'm here and I'm in it up to my ears. I might as well get paid for my headaches."

"Good." Kirk walked back to the decanter and poured himself another drink.

"There's only one if," Liddell told him. "If he's gotten his hands on that half a million, he's probably on the other side of the world by now."

Kirk shook his head. "He hasn't got it. The dough is here in a safe place. The receipt for the box was torn in half. I have half, and Jorges got half. When he was ready to close the deal, we were supposed to get together, put the two halves together. Frederici has only one half of the check. He can't do a thing without the other half." He tossed off the drink, and some of it spilled down his chin.

"Was Frederici working with Jorges on the deal?"

Kirk wiped his chin with the back of his hand and shook his head. "I didn't even know Jorges knew him." He put the cork back into the decanter and walked back to the couch. "Jorges was supposed to deal with me. Frederici had nothing to do with that operation."

177

"Frederici handled the dope for your setup, that it?"

A hard note crept into Kirk's voice. "You find him. Never mind sticking your nose into my business."

Liddell walked past him, went over to the decanter, sniffed it, approved. He poured himself a drink and tasted it. It tasted as good as it smelled. "I'm not blowing any police whistles, Kirk. But I have to know the whole setup before I can handle this. This babe, for instance, where does she set in the picture?"

"Wanda?" Kirk shrugged. "I planted her with Alfred to keep an eye on him. He was a twister from away back. Lou Mendel wished him on me when the coast got too hot to hold him."

Liddell nodded.

"We needed a place to push our quota of the white stuff. He had plenty of experience, came up with the idea of this phony cult. The suckers went for it like flies to honey."

"Wanda's been there since the place opened?"

"She handled the picture end of it. We used infrared and got some shots that were worth their weight in gold."

Liddell nodded. "I know all about that part of it. Get to the part about Alfred fading out."

Kirk cracked his knuckles nervously. "I got word Jorges was coming. I was supposed to contact him a couple of days later. That night, Wanda calls from the temple. They got a houseful of fish and no Alfred. I told her to fake it. It went off so well, we kept it up until the sheriff tipped us off the big heat was going on."

"He was getting his, of course?"

"Plenty. Anyway, when they found this body in Alfred's car, Lalonde wanted to write it right off and get rid of Alfred. Wanda was doing as good or better."

"I saw one of her performances," Liddell grunted.

178

"That's the way it stands. Now you tell me Frederici isn't dead."

Liddell nodded. "I'm almost positive it was Jorges' body. I found his wallet in the Martinez girl's flat after she was murdered."

"Frederici did that, you think?"

"Must have. Martinez found the wallet, the way I figure it. She thought it had something to do with Alfred's disappearance. She was very close to him, wasn't she?"

Kirk nodded. "He kicked her around like a football. She loved it."

"She found this wallet, didn't know where to go with it, so she called me. Somehow, Alfred got wind of it and went up there to shut her up."

"Why are you so sure it was Alfred?"

Liddell shrugged. "It figures. She had found something that she thought related to the death of Alfred. She'd be awfully careful who she let in."

Kirk snorted. "You're just guessing."

Liddell shook his head. "It's more than a guess. Here's a dame that has something she knows is as hot as a fifty-cent pistol. Yet, she's found in her bedroom, stark naked with no signs of a struggle. What does that mean?"

"You're the detective. You tell me."

"It means the killer was either someone with whom she was intimate or someone who had her wrapped around his finger. Either description could fit Alfred."

"But he still left the wallet? The thing he came for?"

"I don't know what happened there," Liddell grunted. "It's a cinch he looked for it. The place was torn apart. But it was well hidden. She had it taped to the underside of the sink in the bathroom. He probably shook the place down as long as he dared, then figured it wasn't there and lit out."

179

"What are you going to do now?"

Liddell drained his glass, set it down on the cabinet. "I'm not too sure. This Jorges character bothers me. If I knew what his pitch was and where he was connected with Alfred, I might have an idea of where to look for Frederici."

Kirk nodded. "Handle it however you like, but keep in touch. If he's still around, he's going to make a try for me. That's the only way he can get the other half of the stub. It's a try that carries a half a million on the nose, so he won't be fooling when he does."

"O.K. If you want me, contact the hotel and leave word. Don't bother sending the little guy. He's beginning to get in my hair." Liddell walked to the door, stopped with his hand on the knob. "You're leveling with me, aren't you, Kirk?"

The mobster twisted his face into a snarl. "What do you mean?"

"You haven't heard from Frederici?"

Kirk hesitated, then shook his head. "No."

Liddell considered it, didn't look too convinced, shrugged. "It's your skin if you like to go around wearing holes in it." He walked through to the anteroom beyond. Hook sat behind the desk, feet up. Wanda leaned against the wall on the opposite side of the room and scowled as Liddell came out.

"Is it O.K. for me to go in now, or do I have to spend the winter out here?" she demanded sulkily.

Liddell looked to Hook. "What's with her?"

The guard shrugged thin shoulders. "You heard the boss. Nobody gets in, he says. To me that means nobody."

Wanda crossed to the door, stopped outside it, studied

180

Liddell from heavy-lidded eyes. "Leo's awful sore at you, Liddell," she told him. "You spoiled his whole day."

Hook chortled loudly. "I saw him, too. And that ain't all you spoiled!"

17.

THE CITY room at the *Dispatch* was getting its breath
between editions when Johnny Liddell walked in. Scraps
of paper, crumpled newspapers, typewriters of varying
vintages, telephones that had lost their luster from con-
stant handling were scattered around the room. A few
men in shirt sleeves, their coats hanging on the backs of
their chairs, were pecking away at typewriters doing
follows on stories that were already on the press.

At other desks, men were sitting back drinking coffee
out of paper containers or just staring ahead getting
their thoughts organized for stories they'd just covered.
Four copy men were working on the rim and two in the
slot slashing copy down to size.

Johnny Liddell worked his way through the desks,
headed for the office Larry Dunlop formerly occupied.
He knocked on the door and walked in. The lean man
looked up from behind the desk where he was checking
through copies of the competitive sheets.

"Hello, Liddell," Eddie Connolly greeted him. His inquisitive gray eyes studied the private detective's face.
"What's new?"

"Nothing, Connolly. I just came by to pay off a debt."

The newspaperman crumpled the paper on his desk,

dumped it into a barrel-sized wastebasket at his elbow. "How's that?"

"Well, when Larry threw in with me, I promised him an exclusive on the Brother Alfred kill. He never got the exclusive."

Connolly shrugged. "That's the way it goes sometimes. Lalonde did such a beautiful cover-up job on that kill, it would have been suicide for us to break that story." He shook his head. "Don't think it didn't eat my guts to have to sit on it. If Larry had been alive, we might have been able to bull it through, but I don't pack his weight."

"Well, I'm paying off on it just the same. I've got that exclusive. This time there won't be any cover-up. In a couple of hours, the F.B.I. will be ready to verify that they've identified Brother Alfred as a west-coast hood on the lam."

The man behind the desk straightened up. "No kidding? Who is he?"

"His name's Al Frederici. Wanted on a couple of counts of murder and dope peddling out there."

"You're sure of this?"

Liddell nodded. "You can check it with Ben Grayson at the local F.B.I. office." He stopped Connolly's grab for the phone with a gesture. "That's not all. The guy in that car wasn't Brother Alfred. He's still alive."

Connolly tugged a phone off its receiver, jabbed at the button on its base. "Tear her down for a page-one remake, Al," he barked into the mouthpiece. "We'll be feeding copy within half an hour. That's right. Get her set up." He deflected the bar on the phone, lifted his finger, jabbed at another button. "Ellis? Get Grayson at the F.B.I. There's a big story out of San Vincente. The guy in that wreck wasn't Brother Alfred, and the F.B.I.

183

is looking for him as Al Frederici." The receiver sputtered back at him. "I don't give a damn how important it is. Drop that and work on the F.B.I. angle. Turn your notes on the transit commission over to Collins." He dropped the receiver on its hook, stared up at the clock, made some lightning estimates. "I can still make the city edition with it," he chortled.

He started rushing toward the door, remembered Liddell, stopped. "Thanks, pal. If Larry were here he'd mark it off Paid in Full. I'll stand in for him on that one. If there's anything we can do for you ever, just yell." He rushed through the door, and Liddell could hear him shouting instructions. The city room dropped its appearance of apathy, was galvanized into feverish activity. Copy boys who were strolling around picking up copy, went scurrying out the door to round up members of the staff.

Connolly came bustling back into his office, slammed the door. He grabbed the phone, raised the composing room. "Set up a scarehead, Tom. Run her ninety point to say 'Cult Leader Exposed as Felon.' Let's have a proof on it right away." He dropped the receiver, seemed surprised to see Liddell was still there.

"Look, Liddell, I don't want to seem ungrateful, but we're bucking a dead line on this one. Can't we get together later?"

Liddell nodded. "I just want some information."

The managing editor's eyes crept up to the face of the clock on the wall. He nodded. "Shoot."

"Ever hear of a man named Ramón Jorges?"

"Jorges, Jorges!" The man behind the desk tasted the word, shook his head. "He a local?"

"A Puerto Rican."

"I never heard of him, but I have a boy who might be
184

able to help you. Wally Paine." His eyes crept back to the clock. "He used to work for INS out of Havana. He's sort of our expert on Caribbean affairs."

"Where can I find him?"

"Around about now he's over at Murphy's Annex across the way. If he's not there, Al the bartender can probably tell you where to find him." He scowled at the clock. "Don't take too much of his time, will you, fellow? I've got a paper to get out." The managing editor started pushing buttons, shouting instructions into the intercom. He had forgotten Johnny Liddell completely —didn't even look up as the door slammed.

Murphy's Annex was an auxiliary city room for the *Dispatch* staff. As Johnny Liddell walked in, the copy boys were herding together the rewrite and feature men who had been leaning against the bar. Liddell walked in, found himself a place at the bar.

"Bourbon and water," he told the bartender.

The bartender filled a jigger, slid it across the bar, and slid a glass with ice and water alongside it. He picked up the bill Liddell dropped, rang it up, and dumped some change on the bar.

"Wally Paine in the place, Al?" Liddell asked.

The bartender stared at him and failed to give any sign of recognition.

"Why?"

Liddell grinned. "I'm not a process server or installment collector. Connolly, his M.E., told me I could find him here."

The bartender thought it over, bought it. He glanced toward the far end of the bar. "The guy with the checked jacket down there." He nodded at a tall, sandy-haired man drinking alone.

Liddell took a swallow from his glass, walked down the bar to where the sandy-haired man stood. "Paine? My name's Liddell. Eddie Connolly over at your shop told me to look you up."

The reporter turned, looked Liddell over. "What can I do for you?"

"I'm trying to run down some information on a guy named Ramón Jorges. He's a Puerto Rican. Ever hear of him?"

"Jorges?" Paine scowled, reached back to the filing cabinet that was his memory. "He's no Riqueno."

"You know him?" Liddell asked eagerly.

Paine rubbed his hand across his face, concentrated. "If it's the same Jorges. What's this guy's racket?"

Liddell shrugged. "I don't know. I just know he's been in Puerto Rico lately."

"He wear thick black-rimmed glasses? Fairly short little gent. Speaks with a Spanish accent?"

"That sounds like him."

Paine grinned, dumped a cigarette from the pack in front of him, got it lighted. "Don't tell me he's running around loose again?"

"He's been around," Liddell hedged.

"Does he still have that Caribbean legion setup?"

Liddell selected a cigarette, took a light from Paine's. "I never heard of it."

"Quite a gimmick," Paine told him. "You know, that little man came damn near creating a real international incident right in our back yard with that Cox's Army of his? Some of them were damn good fighting men, too."

Liddell took a deep drag on his cigarette, added to the slow-moving fog that swirled slowly near the ceiling. "When was this?"

186

Paine stared up at the ceiling, pursed his lips. "Must have been in '47. I was running the INS bureau in Havana in '47 and '48. The story broke about the third month I was down there." He took a swallow from his glass and tapped it on the bar to catch Al's attention. "You don't remember the story?"

Liddell shook his head.

"Well, this Caribbean legion had headquarters at Cayo Confites in Cuba. Everybody thought they were a bunch of crackpots. Drilled every day, all that kind of thing. All of a sudden word got out that they were planning an invasion on the Dominican Republic. They were all set to overthrow Trujillo and set this Jorges up as head man."

"What happened?"

Paine shrugged. "The Cuban Government moved in. They confiscated the legion's invasion fleet, a surplus U.S. landing craft." He grinned. "That was the end of the invasion."

"Make it two, and put it on my check, Al," Liddell told the bartender. He waited until the drinks were poured and Al got busy elsewhere. "What happened to Jorges?"

"This is the first I've heard of him since then," Paine told him. "I guess the confiscation of his LSC just about broke him." He stroked his jaw. "If he's in New Orleans, you don't figure he's cooking up another revolution, do you?"

"What would he be doing here?"

"Hell, there've been more Central American revolutions cooked up at the old Cosmopolitan on Royal Street than anywhere else in the place. Besides, if the legion is being reactivated, he's going to need guns and ammo and maybe even another LSC."

"Here?"

187

Paine nodded. "Here in the Quarter you can outfit a whole revolution from professional soldiers to an airplane carrier. It's the same as in the old days, but today it takes more money."

"Sounds a little bit like Richard Harding Davis, doesn't it? In the old days, a successful revolution paid off plenty in concessions. What would the winners of a revolution get today?"

"Maybe nothing. Maybe it's just a case of Latin politics boiling over again. They have to let off steam every so often." Paine took a deep swallow from his glass, shrugged. "Then, again, some of those Caribbean republics would give a potential enemy a wonderful base of operations within striking distance of all our big cities and the Canal."

Liddell tugged at his earlobe, shook his head. "Maybe our Central Intelligence makes some mistakes, but they'd never let anything slide that close to home."

"I don't think so either." Paine drained his glass and declined a refill. "I've got to get back to the office, or Connolly'll be sending a squad over to get me." He clapped Liddell on the shoulder. "Good to know you, Liddell. If you get to see Jorges, give him my best."

Liddell finished his drink, ordered a refill. He puzzled over what Paine had told him, but the pieces refused to fall into place. Jorges had a half-millon dollars of the syndicate's money, presumably to buy supplies for a revolution. He kicked the presumption around in his mind but rejected it. Certainly, the syndicate wasn't underwriting a revolution to provide a base for the Communists or anybody else to—

It hit him suddenly. He snapped his fingers, grinned tightly.

The phone was in the back of the Annex. He walked

back, fished a coin from his pocket, dropped it in the slot, and dialed Marty Kirk's number. After a moment, Kirk came to the phone.

"I been trying to reach you, Liddell," Kirk complained. "I want you to be here about nine thirty."

"Anything important?"

"Plenty. I heard from Frederici." Kirk's voice seemed to break. "He wants my half of the stub by ten tonight or I get hit."

"You're not giving it to him?"

Kirk laughed dryly. "You crazy? If I got to have somebody on my tail, I'll take Frederici anytime instead of the syndicate's troops." He cleared his throat nervously. "You'll be here?"

"I'll be there. But answer me a question first. Where's Lucky DeLucchio right now?"

The line seemed to go dead. Kirk's voice was husky when he answered. "What kind of a question's that to ask?"

"Where is he, Kirk? This is important."

"In Sicily. He was deported ten years ago. He can't come back."

Liddell nodded. "But he's still top man?"

"Sure he's top man. The board has to report to him on everything. What the hell's that got to do with me?"

"A lot," Liddell assured him. "I just found out what the deal was that Jorges was cooking."

The sound of Kirk's indrawn breath came across the wire. "What?"

"Jorges has a private army all set up. The syndicate was backing him to guns and ammo to pull a revolution in some Caribbean island."

"You gone nuts?" the receiver demanded. "What the hell would they shoot a half a million on that for?"

"Because Lucky's getting pretty tired of sitting it out alone in Sicily, Marty. Awful tired."

"So?"

"So they back this joker on a revolution. If he wins, it's like the old days when the mob took over Cicero outside of Chi. They make their own laws, elect their own officials. Lucky would be allowed to live there, come and go as he pleased a few hours from the United States."

"They wouldn't go to all that trouble just to—"

"It's even juicier than that, Marty. They'd have a base within handy distance of all our big cities and the Canal to shove their narcotics. And it's close enough to Miami, New Orleans, New York, and Chi to set up a gambling casino that would make Monte Carlo look like a penny arcade. And it could operate wide open, Marty."

Marty's voice sounded low. "You're sure of that, Liddell?"

Liddell said yes. "That means that Lucky and the boys are going to be awful upset when they find someone pulled the plug out on their plans by killing Jorges, Marty."

Kirk's voice was almost inaudible. "Yeah. Awful mad."

18.

MARTY KIRK was scared.

It showed in the little twitch under his left eye, the thin film of perspiration that glistened on his upper lip.

"He's bluffing," he said. "Only he picked the wrong guy to bluff." He hit himself on the chest with the side of his hand. "Frederici's crazy to think he can muscle Marty Kirk into a shake."

Wanda looked up from her carefully shellacked fingernails, smiling lazily. "From the way you've been acting the past couple of days you sure could fool me." Tonight her thick wavy black hair cascaded down over her shoulders in shimmering jet waves. Her body was ripe, lush. Swelling breasts showed over the top of her low cut dress; a small waist hinted at the full hips, long shapely legs concealed by the fullness of her skirt. She turned the full force of the slanted green eyes on Liddell. "He hasn't been out of this place in days. He says Alfred's not bluffing him. Look at him shaking apart."

"Shut up, you!" Kirk snarled at her.

Liddell looked over to where his client stood in front of the fireplace, clenching and unclenching his hands.

"How come you didn't tell me before now that somebody's been trying to shake you loose from your half o' the stub?" he wanted to know. "Why wait until the last minute?"

Kirk shrugged. "I thought my boys could handle it. I thought it was Jorges, and we could smoke him out into the open." He spat angrily into the fireplace. "They got no place."

Liddell nodded, looked down at the typewritten sheet he held in his lap. "He wants the stub or you get it by ten tonight." He consulted the watch on his wrist, grinned humorlessly. "That leaves exactly five minutes. I can't do much for you in five minutes if your boys couldn't even get to first base in five days."

"I don't want you to do anything. All I want you to do is stand by for a couple of hours." Kirk wiped the perspiration off his upper lip with the back of his hand. "It ain't that I don't trust my boys, but I like the idea of having a gun handy I can be sure of." He stole a nervous look at the clock on the desk, compared it with the watch on his wrist. "He's bluffing. He's got to be."

The girl snorted, walked over to the big picture window, pushed back the blinds, stared down into the street ten stories below. Kirk started to yell at her, checked himself. With a shrug, he walked over behind her, hands going around her, lips to her neck.

"No need for you hanging around, baby," he told her. "Go on back to your place. I'll talk to you in the morning."

Wanda coolly removed his hands from the front of her strapless grown. "By ouija board?" Her eyes flickered past him, ignored the rush of angry color in his face. "So long, Liddell. I hope you enjoy holding his hand. I'm getting tired of it."

She walked across the room and stopped with her

hand on the knob. "Mind letting me out of this vault, Marty?"

Kirk walked to his desk and jabbed at a concealed button. The door opened, and Hook materialized in the opening. His hand was jammed deep in his bulging pocket, his eyes hopscotched around the room. Finally, they came to rest hungrily on the brunette.

The fullness of her lips straightened out into an angry line. "When you get to the lower rib, Hook, it's really a birthmark."

The guard's eyes narrowed. "What the hell's she talking about?"

"I didn't know you weren't done undressing me," Wanda snapped at him. She turned to look at Marty. "I thought you were going to do something about this jerk looking at me that way."

"No," Kirk told her. "I'm going to do something about you when they stop looking at you that way, baby." He nodded at Hook. "See that somebody puts her in a cab."

The girl stamped through the doorway. The door swung shut behind her.

"That dame's going to drive me screwy. I ain't got enough on my mind, she's got to get particular how a guy looks at her." He wiped his forehead with the flat of his hand, stared at the dampness of his palm. "You figure like me, don't you, Liddell? It's a bluff?"

"Maybe."

"What do you mean, maybe? You think he's crazy enough to think I'll stick my neck in a noose with the big boys just because he talks tough?"

Liddell shrugged. "Maybe whoever wrote that doesn't expect you to kick in. Maybe he's planning on hitting you and using this," he held up the typewritten note, "as a cover."

Kirk's eyes receded behind their discolored pouches. "Go on."

"If you did get it and the mob found this note, they'd be looking for Jorges, figuring like you did that he was behind it." Liddell brought a pack of cigarettes from his pocket, stuck one in the corner of his mouth. "Frederici doesn't know yet that we know who's in that box. Or maybe it isn't Frederici at all."

"What do you mean? Who would it be?"

"Some of your own boys, maybe. Could even be some of your organization who don't like the way things are going—Camden and the temple getting knocked over, things getting out of hand."

Marty watched the private detective apply a match to his cigarette, exhale twin streams of smoke from his nostrils. "That's crazy. They know better than that."

Liddell shrugged. "Then maybe the letter is on the level. Maybe Frederici is putting his whole pile on the line for a winner-take-all roll." He took the cigarette from between his lips, rolled it between thumb and forefinger. "This is just conversation. You said yourself I'm not here to crack this thing in five minutes. I'm just up here to keep you company."

Marty nodded jerkily. "Yeah, that's right." He stole another quick look at the watch on his wrist. "Two minutes to go," he said. "How about a drink, Liddell? I got some of that private stock you like."

"Sounds good to me."

Kirk walked over to his desk and jabbed at the button. The door swung open. Hook's dark head appeared in the opening.

"Bring in a bottle of my private stock, Hook," Kirk told him.

After the door swung shut, Marty drummed on the

edge of the desk with thick fingers, stared at the closed door thoughtfully. "You were just making with the talk when you said it might be some of my boys, weren't you, Liddell?"

"Not entirely. It's a possibility. I don't see how anybody else could hope to get at you." He looked around. "How many ways to get in here?"

"Just that door. The way you came." Kirk walked over, sat on the edge of an upholstered chair facing Liddell. "They'd need a tank to get through there. First they've got to go through the lobby, get past Tim and half a dozen of my boys I got planted around. Then they got to get past Hook, who's planted out front of the door here." Perspiration glistened on his forehead. "Unless Hook's in on it."

"It's been known to happen." Liddell checked his watch, slid his .45 from its holster, rested it between his thigh and the arm of his chair. "He'd be the ideal guy to handle the contract."

"Why should he? The Hook's been with me since I ran the old Variety Club over in the Quarter. That's twenty years ago. Why should he want to see me hit?"

"Who knows? You saw the way he looked at the babe. Maybe he figures he'll rate if you're not in the way. Maybe he figures—"

Marty's jaw sagged. He jumped up, paced the room. "You're nuts." He stopped in front of Liddell's chair. "He wouldn't pull anything like that. Just for a dame!"

"Not only for the dame, Marty. No guy likes to stay Number Two boy all his life. You were Number Two boy in this town once. Seems to me your boss met with a bad accident. His tough luck was your good luck."

Kirk's face clouded ominously. Some of the old menace gleamed through the slitted eyelids. "He got soft. He
195

didn't rate—" He broke off as the door opened and the bodyguard entered with a bottle, two glasses, and some ice. Kirk's eyes followed the small man as he crossed the room, set down the tray. "Pour it, Hook."

The guard dropped two pieces of ice into each glass, drenched them down with whisky from an unlabeled bottle.

"Ever try that private stock of mine, Hook?" Kirk asked silkily.

The thin man looked startled, rolled his eyes upward without raising his head. "You give us all orders to keep our hands off. Regular whisky's good enough for me." He picked up the glasses, held one out to Liddell, the other to Kirk. His eyes didn't change expression as he saw the .45 Liddell cradled carelessly in his lap.

"Try it once, Hook," Kirk told him.

The bodyguard looked from Marty to Liddell and back. "What's the idea, boss?"

"Try it." Kirk's voice was edged, harsh.

The thin man shrugged. "O.K." He put one glass back on the desk, raised the other to his lips. He sniffed at it for a second, then, tilting his head back, he drained the glass. His thin lips tilted upward at the corners in what he intended as a smile as he reached to set the glass back on the desk.

He never made it.

His body seemed to stiffen. He laced both hands against his mid-section, stretched up on his toes. Then slowly his knees buckled, tumbling him to the floor.

Liddell was out of his chair in a second, kneeling beside the fallen man. Marty seemed frozen to the spot. "The rat! It was him. He tried to poison me!"

Liddell looked up, shook his head. "Not unless that stuff's sharper than it was in the old days. He's bleeding." He pointed to a rapidly spreading dark spot on the front of Hook's jacket.

"Bleeding? How the hell can that be?" Marty walked over, stared down at the body.

"Get back!" Liddell shouted.

There was a faint hum of an angry bee. Marty jerked his hands to his face. Red started to trickle through the fingers. He pitched forward and hit the floor face down. He didn't move.

Liddell flattened himself against the floor, tugged the .45 from Hook's pocket, wormed his way to the window. He applied a cautious eye to the corner and tried to locate the source of the shots.

Directly across the street were a hotel, a huge modern office building, and on the corner a department store. He eliminated the hotel as not being high enough and the department store as unlikely, settled for the office building. He leaned the barrel of the .45 on the window sill, watched, waited.

He didn't have long to wait. In a matter of seconds, a dark shadow separated itself from the other shadows, headed for the edge of the roof. Finally, a man's leg appeared over the edge and felt for the top landing of the fire escape. Then the rest of the body came into view. The man peered over the railing to the alley below, seemed satisfied, started down the stairs.

Liddell waited until the upper portion of the man's body sat on the front sight of his .45, then squeezed the trigger. The boom of the .45 was deafening in the close confines of the soundproofed room.

Across the street, the man on the fire escape staggered. He tried to get back to the roof, stumbled to his knees. Slowly, he managed to pull himself to his feet, stood swaying. Liddell's .45 barked again.

The man on the fire escape stiffened, clawed at the guard rail. His knees folded under him. He toppled over the low rail, crashed headlong to the alley below.

Liddell knelt with his eye glued to the window until he was satisfied that the gunman across the way had been alone. Then he walked back to where Marty lay, turned him over on his back. A blue-black hole that was still bubbling under his right eye made it apparent that he was beyond help.

The private detective debated the advisability of reporting the shooting to the police, lost the decision. He was too close to the end of the twisting trail to be detoured by police procedure. He wiped Hook's .45 clean and dropped it alongside the dead bodyguard's body. He picked his up from his chair and stuck it in its holster. Then he headed for the street.

The street was cool after the closeness of Marty's penthouse. The cross streets were filled with heavy after-dinner traffic, but the square was relatively deserted. Liddell crossed the street and blended into the shadows of the tall office building. When he had satisfied himself that he was unobserved, he slipped into the alley that ran alongside it.

The man was spread-eagled over a stack of garbage cans. Lying nearby, its stock shattered by the fall, was a high-powered rifle equipped with telescopic sights and silencer. Liddell leaned over the man's face, studied his features, failed to recognize him. Imported talent.

Quickly, efficiently, he ran through the man's pockets and transferred the wallet, a few papers, and a key with a small red tag into his own pockets.

Then he retraced his steps up the alley, swung onto the avenue, and headed for a cab.

19.

THREE HOURS later, Johnny Liddell sat at the table in his hotel apartment and scowled at the small pile in front of him. The dead sniper's wallet had given him nothing aside from the man's name and an address in Los Angeles, neither of which meant anything to him. A few decks of heroin secreted in an inner compartment of the wallet testified to the fact that he was a professional killer; the six one-hundred-dollar bills to the fact that he was a highly paid expert.

Liddell picked up the folded piece of notepaper, reread it for the third time. "Check into Carlyle Apartments in New Orleans under the name of William Wellington. The enclosed $400 will pay for your trouble. If I still need you, I'll know where to reach you and the other $600 and your instructions will be delivered by messenger before you do the job." It was unsigned.

Liddell pulled from his pocket the typewritten note Marty Kirk had received. He compared the typing and was satisfied that both had been done on the same machine. He leaned back, raked his fingers through his hair, and swore under his breath. He was at a dead end—the sniper apparently had no more idea of where the man who hired him could be found than Liddell had.

The telephone at his elbow shrilled. He contemplated the advisability of not answering it, finally scooped the receiver from its cradle.

"Liddell?" The voice was low, husky, disturbing.

"Who's this?"

"Wanda. Marty's girl. I'm downstairs in the lobby." She paused for a moment, seemed to be taking a deep breath. "I've got to see you. Can I come up?"

"Come ahead. I'm in room three-forty." He dropped the receiver back on its hook, staring at it speculatively. Then he picked up the wallet, the tagged key, and the typewritten notes, dropped them into his jacket pocket, and hung it in the closet. He looked around, scowled at the bright overhead light, snapped it out, and turned on the bridge lamp over the armchair.

Then he lifted the phone, asked for the house detective, waited until McGinnis answered. "See the girl that just called me on the house phone, Mac?"

There was a long, low, appreciative whistle from the other end of the wire.

"She alone when she came in?" Liddell asked.

"All alone. She headed for the desk, asked if you were in. The clerk gave me the high sign, and I gave him the nod. I hope it was O.K." A worried note crept into the house man's voice. "Hell, I didn't think anybody would mind if a babe like that—"

"She didn't talk to anybody after she called me?"

"There was nobody else but me in the lobby. She walked right from the booth to the elevator. I don't mind telling you I couldn't take my eyes off her from the minute she—"

There was a knock on the door.

"O.K., Mac. That's all I wanted to know." Liddell

dropped the receiver back on the hook, walked to the door, and pulled it open.

She was even more breath-taking than earlier. The thick blue black hair was piled on top of her head. Her face was scrubbed clean of make-up as it had been the first night he saw her at the temple. Tonight, though, she wore a red smear of lipstick on her full lips. She wore a full-length camel's-hair polo coat, no stockings, a pair of loafers.

She walked past him into the room and waited until he had closed the door behind her. "Lock it," she said in a low voice.

Liddell snapped the lock. "What's it all about?"

"Marty. Alfred got him just like he said he would, didn't he? What happened? You were there. You must have seen it."

Liddell nodded. "He planted a sharpshooter with a reacher—"

"A reacher?"

"A silenced rifle with a telescopic-lens setup. It was like shooting sitting ducks. He got Hook, too, you know." He led the way to the couch. "Sit down and catch your breath." She stood uncertainly in the middle of the floor.

When he helped her off with her coat, he whistled noiselessly. Under the camel's hair coat she wore only a pair of light blue silk pajamas, the trouser legs rolled up to her knees.

"I was ready for bed when the call came from Leo. I was too scared to take the time to dress. I just grabbed a coat and ran." She walked closer to him, put her hands on his chest. "I didn't know where else to go, Johnny." Her full lower lip trembled. "Poor Marty. I thought he was just cracking up, seeing bogymen in the shadows.

Don't let Alfred get me the way he got Marty, Liddell."

"Why should he want to kill you?" Liddell fought to keep his glance at face level, lost the struggle.

"I worked pretty close with Alfred. He might be afraid I know where he's hiding out."

"Do you?"

The girl's face went a shade whiter. She wet her lips with the tip of a pink tongue. "He has a hide-out on the old Bayou St. Jacques road. That's where he was holed up when he lit out of the temple."

Liddell nodded thoughtfully. "Why didn't you tell Marty this?"

"I don't know. I guess I felt a little sorry for Alfred." She dropped her arms, walked to the window, and looked out. "I thought he was a little crazy. He was going to do such big things—take over Marty's operation. Everything, me included. He said Marty was getting soft." She swung around. "I thought it was just talking. I didn't believe he could do it or that he'd even try." As she walked back toward him, the sway of her breasts traced designs on the shiny silk of her pajama jacket. "He knows I know all that." She shuddered, massaged the back of her arms with her palms. "Got a drink handy?"

Liddell nodded, walked into the kitchenette, and came back with a bottle and two glasses. He spilled some liquor into each of the glasses and passed one to the girl.

"When you spoke to Marty's boys, did they tell you whether they found the guy who picked off Marty?"

The girl took a deep swallow from her glass, shook her head. "He was probably a hired gun. They'll never find him."

Liddell grinned glumly. "Don't make any book on that, baby. They can't miss him."

She stopped with her glass halfway to her lips. "What do you mean?"

"I picked him off the roof across the street with Hook's forty-five. He's spilled all over the alley next to the office building facing Marty's place." He dropped down on the couch alongside her. "He was outside talent. Brought in from L.A. especially for this job."

Her mouth was an O of amazement. "You went up against him with a forty-five and him using a rifle with telescopic sights?" She moved closer. "No wonder Marty went running to you when things started getting too deep. I'm glad I came."

"I didn't do Marty much good. He's dead."

"But you got the guy who did it." She leaned back against the couch, strained her high, tip-tilted breasts against the fragile pajama fabric, and stared at him in open admiration. "Just like that. You picked him off the roof with a forty-five." Her eyelids half veiled the green of her eyes; she studied him through the long lashes. "I could never pay you what you're worth to protect me, but I'd try to make it worth your while." She leaned close to him, her breath warm, fragrant on his cheek. He was aware of the disturbing smell of her hair, her body. "Let me stay here tonight, Johnny. I don't want to go home. I'm afraid."

"O.K., baby. Make yourself at home." He leaned over, found her lips with his. They clung for a moment, then she put the flat of her hands against his chest, pushed him away.

"Do we need all that light?" She pulled herself to her feet, walked to the lamp.

"I wasn't kidding poor Hook. I do have a birthmark on my bottom rib." She pulled the blouse of her pajamas high enough to reveal a strawberry-shaped blemish on the whiteness of her body. She dropped the blouse, fumbled with the zipper on the pajamas, snapped the light off.

From where he sat, Liddell could hear the soft rustle of the silk as she slid out of the pajamas. Then she straightened up. The whiteness of her body gleamed in the reflected light from the window. Her legs were long, sensuously shaped. Full, rounded thighs swelled into high-set hips, converged into the narrow waist he had admired earlier in the evening. Her breasts were full and high, their pink tips straining upward.

As she stood there, she raised her hands slowly from her sides and loosened the pile of hair on her head, letting it cascade down over her shoulders. It gleamed in the faint light.

She padded across the room, stood proudly in front of Liddell.

The luminous hands of the clock set next to the bed pointed to 4:10. The girl stirred uneasily, opened her eyes, stared around in the unfamiliar darkness. Suddenly, she sprang to wide-eyed wakefulness, sat up, and pulled the blanket around her. "Liddell! Liddell! Where are you?" she called.

The door to the bathroom beyond opened, spilling a triangle of yellow light into the darkened living room. Liddell walked in, drying his still damp hair. He was dressed except for his shirt and tie. "Shower wake you, baby? Sorry. You go on back to sleep."

"You're going to leave me here alone?"

"I've got something I've got to do. You'll be all right here. Just don't answer any telephone calls or open the door."

"Where are you going?"

Liddell balled the damp towel and tossed it at the open bathroom door. "To see Alfred. There are a couple of things I want cleared up before I hand him over to Homicide."

The brunette dropped the blanket, stood up. "Be careful, Johnny. He's a killer. Don't stick your neck out."

Liddell pecked at her cheek. "Look, baby. Marty wasn't much of a guy. His being hit was no loss to the community. But he was my client, and I don't like people who knock off my clients."

Wanda shook her head helplessly. "I wish you wouldn't go."

"I won't be long, baby." He lifted his shoulder harness from a peg in the closet, adjusted it, and covered it with his jacket. "The Bayou St. Jacques road, you said. What's the place look like?"

The girl dropped her eyes. "I've never been there. He kept asking me to come, but I never did."

"Didn't he tell you how to find the place?"

Wanda looked up at him and nodded. "It's a little shack set back off the right-hand side of the road. It's about two miles past the highway crossroads. There's a picket fence around it. There are no other houses near there."

Liddell nodded. "I'll find it. Don't forget what I said. Don't answer the phone or open the door. For anybody."

She nodded, slid arms around his neck, and pressed her body close to his.

20.

THE SHACK stood about a hundred feet off the Bayou St. Jacques road. It was surrounded by a decayed picket fence from which most of the pickets had fallen to rot in the weed-choked front yard. Johnny Liddell drove the rented car past the house, swung it off the road, parked it behind an old moss-bearing oak. He turned off his lights and sat for a moment. There was no sound but the distant hum of some insect.

He got out of the car and followed a badly overgrown path to the doorway. The steps creaked under him as he climbed to the porch. There was no light in the house, no sign of life. Liddell tried the doorknob softly, found it locked, and brought out a handful of keys. The third one he tried opened the door. The room beyond was in pitch darkness.

Liddell stepped in and closed the door behind him. He had the eerie, uncomfortable feeling that he wasn't alone in the room. He squinted into the darkness, strained his ear for some sound that would betray the presence of someone else. There was no sound.

After a moment, Liddell slid his hand along the wall until he felt the light switch. He pressed the switch, throwing the room into sudden, blinding light. Simultaneously, he dropped to his knee, his .45 at ready.

Al Frederici, the pseudo Brother Alfred, sat in a large armchair not ten feet away, staring at him with unblinking eyes. He no longer wore the black beard or white robe in his disguise as Alfred and looked more like the pictures on the F.B.I. B.I. card. His holster, with a snub-nosed automatic nestling in it, hung over the back of his chair, the gun butt less than a foot from his hand.

Liddell got up and walked over to where Alfred sat. He bent over him, examined the three little dark holes that had ripped through from the back of his head spilling a cascade of red down his shirt.

Liddell scowled, straightened up, looked around. On the table at the dead man's elbow there was a bowl of melted ice, two glasses half full of brown liquid.

He put his fingers inside a glass, spread them out until he could lift the glass without defacing the prints on the outside. Then he breathed on the outside of the glass.

There was no sign of a print.

He repeated the procedure with the other glass, found a full set of prints.

"That's a big help," he growled. "The killer wore gloves." He was about to set the glass back on the table when he heard a car skidding to a stop. Quickly, he crossed to the switch, doused the light, wiped off any possible prints with his handkerchief.

He pulled aside the corner of the blind and looked out. A police car had pulled up in front of the house. The door opened, Sheriff Lalonde of San Vincente hopped out, riot gun in hand. He looked around, then started up the path to the house.

Liddell crossed the room and pushed up the sash of the window on the far side. He threw one leg over the sill and had just cleared the window when the front door was kicked open.

He ran across the weed-choked yard toward where he had left his car. Suddenly, a man's head appeared in the window he had just come through. Liddell kept going, made the shelter of the big oak. There was a series of sharp bangs from behind; buzzing slugs bit chunks out of the bark of the tree over his head. Liddell dropped to his knees and made for the car.

It seemed like an eternity before the motor roared into life. He threw the car into gear and headed back for the road. As he swung onto the road, a figure materialized in the glare of his headlights. He stood with legs planted apart, riot gun in his hand.

Liddell jammed on the brake, skidded the car to a stop. Lalonde stood in the beam of the headlights, leering at him. "I told you we'd be meeting again, shamus," he raised the riot gun, "but this is the last time."

"O.K., sheriff. I didn't kill him and you know it. But I'll go along." Liddell raised his hands.

The sheriff shook his head. "I'm not taking you alive, Liddell. You're too smooth a talker. You might talk your way out of it. This time I'm making sure." He had the riot gun almost at his shoulder.

"You can't get away with it, sheriff," Liddell yelled.

"Any peace officer has the right to blast a killer who tries to escape."

Liddell slipped his foot off the brake.

The riot gun in Lalonde's hands started to belch orange flame. The windshield fell to pieces around Liddell, as he jammed his foot down on the gas pedal. The big car roared, jumped ahead, sprang at the man in the road like a living thing. He stood there, squeezing the trigger.

Liddell had a momentary view of the sheriff's face across the top of the hood. His mouth was open, and he was screaming something. The full-throated roar of the motor drowned him out.

There was a faint jar, then the road was empty in the glare of the headlights. Liddell jammed on the brakes, ran back to where the sheriff lay in the middle of the road.

He was on his back, one leg folded crazily under him. The riot gun lay alongside his outstretched hand.

Liddell bent down, felt for his pulse. There was none.

The brunette started, looked up wide-eyed as Johnny Liddell let himself back into his apartment. He ignored the question in her eyes, headed for the end table, and poured himself a stiff drink from the bottle.

"What's happened? Alfred isn't—"

Liddell repeated the prescription, nodded. "Dead. Shot through the back of his head." He set the glass down, wiped his mouth. "The half of the stub he got from Jorges is probably gone too."

"I don't get it," the brunette shook her head. "All the time I thought it was Alfred behind it. It figured to be."

Liddell shucked his jacket, slid out of his shoulder holster, and threw it on the couch. "It looks like it's a neat package now. Alfred's dead for real this time. Kirk's dead, the sniper's dead, and Marty's bodyguard has a half-emptied magazine to prove he died protecting his boss."

He walked over to his window, stared out. "Just for good measure, your friend the sheriff over in San Vincente is dead, too."

"I—I don't know what you mean, Johnny."

Liddell didn't turn around. "Marty was through with you, wasn't he, Wanda? He was getting set to throw you out, and you didn't like it. He must have been, or he wouldn't let that little gun slinger of his look at you like you were a piece of beef. When Marty's through with you, there's not a lot you can do about it, is there, baby?" He didn't wait for her answer. "You weren't going to stand still for it, were you?"

The girl shook her head and couldn't seem to frame words with her lips.

"You knew about Jorges and the two halves of the stub to get the five hundred thousand. You had an idea and sold it to Alfred."

"I didn't, Johnny. You're wrong. I—"

"It had to be someone real close to Marty. Someone who knew just how soft he really was. It wasn't Hook, or he wouldn't have stood there and taken that one in the belly. You figured that if you had one half of the stub you could muscle the other half out of Marty. You didn't realize he was more scared of the big boys than he was of getting killed."

The brunette caught her lower lip between her teeth, chewed it.

"All right," she said. "I did plan to break away from Marty. I told Alfred about the five hundred thousand. He wanted to try for it." She caught him by the arm. "You knew Marty—he was fixing to swing me into that stable of hustlers of his, shipping me around the country like I was cattle or something. I told Alfred how easy it would be to scare Marty. But that's all I intended. Just to scare him. I didn't know about the guy with the rifle."

She walked over to the couch and helped herself to a drink. "The first I knew about it was when they called

210

me to tell me Marty was dead. I rushed out to Alfred's place to find out what was going on, and he was dead, too. I was scared, so I came here."

"You're a liar. You knew all about the guy with the rifle. You even opened the curtains on the window and gave him the signal."

"You can't prove that, Liddell."

"I don't have to. They can only burn you once—for killing Alfred. And they'll have no trouble proving you did that."

"How?"

Liddell shrugged. "You signed your name to it. Alfred was drinking with whoever killed him, but the killer was wearing gloves. It had to be a woman."

"Why?"

"Because a gun-smart hood like Alfred, going up against a killer like Marty Kirk, even a softened-up Marty Kirk, would never let anyone but a woman get that close to him wearing gloves. You probably even wore the gloves home and left them there to be found with the powder burns on them."

"Who have you told this to, Johnny?"

Liddell shrugged. "No one—yet."

"You wouldn't turn me in, Johnny. Not now. Not after we—"

"Turn it off, baby. You set me up for the kill, too, when you set Marty up. You signaled your boy with the reacher to take two. You couldn't have known that Hook would be in the room just at ten. Your boy took care of two, thought he was finished for the night. He was—for good."

The girl sobbed deep in her throat. "Even if that were true, I didn't know you then. I couldn't have—"

"Is that why you tried to put me on the spot for Sheriff

Lalonde? He knew I was there, Wanda, came for me with a riot gun. He wasn't looking for a pinch—he wanted me dead. You set it up."

"I didn't!"

"It had to be you. You were the only one who knew I was out there. Only the person who killed Alfred could have known what I would find. You tipped Lalonde so he could catch me with a body on my hands and have some justification for burning me down before he took me in."

Wanda shook her head. "No, Johnny. You're wrong."

"I checked the switchboard on the way in, baby," he growled. "You made a call while I was gone." He took a deep breath. "That wasn't smart."

"Maybe I didn't care. Maybe I was sure you weren't coming back." There was a new note in Wanda's voice. "Turn around, Liddell. I want you to see it coming."

Liddell turned from the window. The brunette had taken his gun from its holster and held it with its muzzle pointing at Liddell's mid-section. "I guess it's like they say. If you want a thing done, do it yourself."

"Then it's all true, baby?"

"You're smarter than I gave you credit for being, Liddell," the girl nodded. "Jorges called one day when Marty was out. He told me where Marty was to contact him. Instead, Alfred and I went over. We got an awful jolt when we found out he had only half the stub. Then we started putting the pressure on Marty for his half."

"That's when I got into the act, eh?" Liddell nodded.

The brunette tossed her head angrily. "I knew you were bad medicine from the minute I found you lifted the glass out of the temple. I wanted to get rid of you, but when Al muffed it from the window, he got cold feet. He tried to play it smart. He put on that disappear-

212

ing act for you out at the park. I should have killed you then and had it over with."

Liddell rubbed the back of his head. "You were the one that sapped me? It was a real professional job."

"It was a pleasure."

"What was the idea of the staged accident?"

Wanda shrugged. "Everybody was supposed to figure Alfred was burned in the wreck. I even identified him. That was your signal to go home and take your nose out of our business."

Liddell stared at the back maw of the .45. "That was the wrong way to do it, baby."

"We made mistakes," the brunette conceded. "Not only with you, but with others. That bucktoothed little Martinez snooping around found Jorges' wallet. That could have been dangerous."

Liddell nodded. "How'd you know about it?"

"Your girl friend, Gabby," Wanda told him. "She found out Martinez was trying to get in touch with you, so she called Marty to tip him off. Only Marty didn't get the message. I did. Alfred paid her a visit." She made a gesture across her throat. "He corrected that mistake."

"And then you killed him."

The brunette shrugged. "I had no choice. He started to turn yellow. When Marty didn't crack like we thought he would, he wanted to take off. He wanted me to go with him. Can you imagine? He actually thought I was trading Marty in for him even. Yeah, we made lots of mistakes."

"You're still making them, baby. Where do you go from here?"

The full lips split in a taunting grin. "Paradise. I've got Jorges' half of the stub, and I know where Marty kept his half. With a half a million dollars I can really go, Liddell." Her finger tightened on the trigger. "But before I go, I'm correcting the biggest mistake of all. You." Her finger whitened on the trigger. "Say hello to Marty and Alfred for me, Liddell." She clenched her teeth, started squeezing the trigger.

The .45 clicked metallically.

"It shoots better with bullets in it," Liddell told her.

Wanda stared at the empty gun and offered no resistance when he walked over and wrenched it from her hand.

She wet the soft lips with the tip of her tongue, flung her hands around his neck, and clung to him. "I didn't mean it, Johnny," she said. "I couldn't have done it."

He held her out at arm's length. The green, almond-shaped eyes were dimmed with tears; her full lips trembled.

"We can have so much together. We can go away. With a half million, we can have everything."

Johnny Liddell stood there, drinking in the pure beauty of her face and body. Mentally, he counted off the men whose deaths lay at her door.

He raised his hand, hit her across the face with the flat of his palm, and knocked her sprawling. She lay there quietly, a thin trickle of blood running down her chin as he walked across the room, lifted the receiver from its hook, and asked the operator for Homicide.